W9-AHB-029

Beam Me Up, Scotty

Beam Me Up, Scotty

A Novel by
Michael Guinzburg

Arcade Publishing • New York

Library of Congress Cataloging-in-Publication Data

Guinzburg, Michael.
    Beam me up, Scotty : a novel / Michael Guinzburg.
        p.   cm.
    ISBN 1-55970-208-7
    I. Title.
    PS3557.U38B4 1993
    813' .54 — dc20   92-54827

Published in the United States by Arcade Publishing, Inc., New York

Distributed by Little, Brown and Company

10 9 8 7 6 5 4 3 2 1

PRINTED IN THE UNITED STATES OF AMERICA

There is a crack in his head that rain will not fill.
— Randall Watson

Beam Me Up, Scotty

My name is Ed, and I'm a stupid stinking drug addict and alcoholic.

When I landed home, drug-free at last, and saw the apartment empty, no wife or kids, clothes and suitcases gone, the old sickness was upon me, polluting my innards with a poisonous mixture of rage and nausea, like hydrogen peroxide bubbling angry white on an open wound. What had I expected? Happy smiley faces and a cake? A brass band? Michelle in a drum majorette uniform over lacy lingerie? Open arms and forgiveness? The eleven-year-old twin boys turning cartwheels? My senile mother out of the nursing home, clearheaded and young again? My father back from the grave? I don't know. Maybe just a cup of hot chocolate and a hug. Certainly not an abandoned apartment with windows wide open to the winter wind.

Down the stairs. Catbox stink of stale piss and vomit. Dead-soldier crack vials crunching undersneaker. Bare bulbs spilling sour lemon light onto hairy dust balls skittering along the grimy hall like urban tumbleweeds. A bum toilet. A junkie Jiffy Lube. A helluva place to raise a family.

1

Outside. Intersection of Bowery and Houston. Spindle-shanked winos wiped windshields, begged change.

Just one whiskey, just one whiskey, I thought, to drown this dreary bastard resentment thrashing in my guts.

I walked the Sunday streets. Frozen air chilled my ears, nipped my nose. The city domed by a clear blue sky, the kind of day an Indian dreams of dying on — the sky so clean and crisp and blue the freshly freed soul just sort of zooms to the heavens.

The Lower East Side one huge sprawling drug bazaar. Streets choked with dealers. Junkies and crackheads paced and lounged, guzzling brown-bagged beers, huffing cigarettes. I couldn't escape the eyes. The hard dull eyes. Empty of everything save the deathgreed. Vultures. "Crack it up!" croaked one. "Jumbo!" said another. "How many you need?" As if they knew I'd gone straight. Teasing me, tempting me, mocking the fact that I was clean. They wanted me back with them, down and dirty, strung out, waltzing with Lucifer, dying slow and living like a zombie on the streets of Crack City, U.S.A.

I hated them. Jumpy jittery bastards. Ready to pop off at any moment. They'd do anything to keep the glass pipe packed with white rock, to stay wired: lie, cheat, steal, murder — sell their mother's wedding ring, trade their baby sister's virginity, their blind uncle's guide dog and sunglasses. They'd do anything, say anything, anything at all for that next mammoth suck off the Devil's Dick.

I hated what crack did to me. What I did for crack. How low I sank into the slime. The snarling animal I became. For the love of crack. For the hot electric cocaine zap. The raging selfish bastard. How I lost my wife and kids, infected them with my disease. I hated myself for that.

I kicked an empty crack vial. It spun into the gutter.

A long time ago in a galaxy far, far away . . . I was a reporter. A bright fresh face with a bright fresh talent, a bright fresh family, and a bright fresh future. My career had wings. That was B.C. (before crack), before the drugs got me by the short hairs and I took a swan dive into the toilet, a pigeon pecking at scraps. "You coulda won the Pulitzer," my friend Ken once mused, cokesmoke billowing from his mouth, passing me the wicked stem. Isn't it pretty to think so?

This, then, is the story of my life after detox (A.D.), where I'd crawled on my knees, moaning and squawking like a cockatoo with a jalapeño pepper jammed up its ass, a prisoner of crack.

I couldn't blame Michelle. I put her through hell. Put them all through hell.

Just one whiskey, just one whiskey, to unravel the pain, make me sane, to uncurdle the sour-milk stink in my heart and brain.

I don't know how long I wandered like that. I smoked a bunch of cigarettes, sucked them down hard, walked until my nose and toes and ears were frozen numb.

A warm smoky East Village church basement crowded with laughing happy people. Clear eyes and clean clothes. After all the years of wildlife it had come to this. Hard Drugs Anonymous. "When you feel like getting high — and you will feel like getting high — go to a meeting." That's what the counselor told me back at detox.

I sat on a hard chair and drank black coffee, smoked a cigarette. The speaker up front leading the meeting, blond and pretty, sitting behind a podium on a raised platform facing the crowd, told the story of her life, how a bottle of Boone's Farm apple wine guzzled in a New England graveyard at age fifteen transformed a cheerleading straight-A student into a pill-popping, vodka-guzzling coke freak who ran off to the big city to make it as an actress, became a junkie-hooker, blew businessmen in cars, got beaten by pimps, stole, turned tricks in stairwells and cars, shot coke and dope time and again until her whole body was freckled with needle tracks, until her veins were clogged, until she was hitting up in the neck, until she hated herself and wanted to die — and now she could sit there, so elegant and serene, so at ease before these laugh-happy strangers, and joke about the horror.

"The disease of addiction is progressive," she said. "How could I have known way back when that an innocent bottle of wine would propel this Suzie Creamcheese on a ten-year run that ended in the back seat of a Mercedes when I realized the guy I was going down on was my Uncle Claude? The shame I felt. That's when I hit bottom, got into treatment, and ended up here, in the rooms of HDA. And I keep coming back, because it's the only way I know to work on myself, to feel my feelings instead of stuffing them with drugs and alcohol, to arrest my disease, one day at a time."

They gave her a nice round of applause, passed the basket, made announcements, then went to a show of hands.

I shot my nicotine-stained mitt into the air. She pointed at me. Must've had a radar for pain.

"My name is Ed, and I'm a stupid stinking drug addict and alcoholic."

"Hi, Ed!" chorused the joyous recovering boozers and addicts.

"I got out of detox today. My fucking wife has taken off. I thought if I got clean, things would get better. But I feel like fried dogshit on a bun. I want to drink or do some dope or smoke some crack so bad I can taste it. The bitch stole my kids. I'd like to kill her."

"Thanks for sharing that, Ed," chirped Miss Happy-face with a shit-eating grin. "It gets better. Give time time. Keep it simple, stupid. Easy does it. One day at a time. Get a sponsor, someone you can talk with about those feelings. Don't stuff them. Keep coming back. The HDA Center has meetings all day and night. About your wife? Don't beat yourself up about it. Listen to learn and learn to listen."

I listened. People spilling their guts: pain, hope, doubt, joy, dreams, demons — psychotherapy for the psychotic masses. When the hour was up we all linked hands and prayed. The AC/DC currents of hope and despair flowed through me.

Between meetings the anonymous boozers and junkies welcomed me. "Thanks for sharing." "You're in the right place." "Take my phone number." "Keep coming back." "Don't stuff those feelings." "Have some coffee." Fuckups of all ages, all races, all manner of dress and demeanor, thanked me for my honesty and told me, "Don't beat yourself up about it." "Give time time." "Hang in there."

I was overwhelmed. Who the fuck was I? Just some piece
of shit scraped off the street. Warm hands pressed mine.
An old guy smiled. A beautiful brunette, straight from
a girlie magazine, crushed me to her bountiful breast,
whispered, "I know how you feel." It had been ages since
I felt so safe, so warm, so at home. So I stayed, through
the afternoon and long into the night, soaking up meetings like a Miami codger takes the sun, studying the faces,
downing coffee, smiling at strangers.

"My name is Myron," said the speaker leading the
last meeting of the night, a middle-aged man in a tasteful
tweed skirt and a white silk blouse, "and I'm a grateful
recovering alcoholic."

"Hi, Myron!" we chimed.

"Alcohol is one of the hardest drugs of all, and I let
it beat me up for twenty-five years. I've always been a
woman inside. I've known that since I was two. I thought
like a woman, felt like a woman, had a woman's intuition
and emotions, but I lived in a man's body. Now I take
hormones and go to therapy to prepare myself for the
eventual operation. When I get this silly old troublemaker
between my legs chopped off, then I'll be happy and
proud to call myself Myra. Of course it will cost a bundle,
so I'm saving up, one day at a time."

Yes, I thought, yes! This is beautiful. A man who
feels like a woman and has the balls to do something
about it! What a glorious program! It allows people to
be who they really are. Yes! And no one is laughing. Not
that rough-looking fuck over there with the black hair
and the permanent five o'clock shadow who looks like he
wouldn't know a feeling if it kicked him in the crackers —
he's nodding right along. And those bikers in the front

row, they're down with Myron too. And that sweet thang who hugged me earlier — she's crying! And that filthy red-haired guy in the corner who was muttering all through the last meeting — he's quiet now, listening. The old lady; the bald-headed guy with the briefcase; the Native American with his cowboy hat and shitkicker boots; the yuppie couple over there with the matching corduroys and button-down shirts; the black woman with the dreadlocks; the —

"Growing up as Myron was no fun. It felt all wrong. Other boys played ball; I played house. I was different. Little girls teased me. My father beat me. I became withdrawn. I played with my sister's dolls and dressed in my mother's clothes. When I was twelve I was raped. I felt worthless, horrible. That night I discovered alcohol, and it helped the pain. From the beginning I drank to get drunk. I loved the warm glow, the feeling of safety. When I was loaded it was okay to be Myra. With others I had to wear a mask.

"At nineteen I got married. I functioned as a man physically, and yeah, I enjoyed it; but the booze was always there. I was drunk all the time. Had three kids, my own dress shop; but trouble was nipping at my heels. One night my wife came to the shop and found me passed out, wearing a lovely little yellow number from the spring line. Divorce, humiliation: the works. I drank more and more, went over that invisible line and kept on falling deeper and deeper into the abyss. I was so numb I didn't even know I was in pain. My real feelings were stuffed so deep and I was in such denial that if you told me I had a problem I'd laugh in your face. For years I lived on the Bowery in a so-called room. A cage with walls. I drank wine and vodka. Gave blowjobs for cash. Finally I couldn't even do that without throwing up, so I ended up on the street, living in a cardboard box. Couldn't afford vodka or wine, so I drank gasoline. That's right, gas. High-octane, regular, unleaded — I cherished them all. I hung around the pumps and begged. I mixed my gas with ginger ale, called my cardboard box the Gas Chamber. Y'see, I was raised Jewish and I thought that was funny. Ha ha ha. That box was my personal Auschwitz, my prison, my coffin, where I was slowly fucking killing myself. Numerous times the cops picked me up, freezing or puking or bleeding or comatose, and they'd drag me fighting and screaming and complaining to countless emergency rooms to have my stomach pumped out. And every time, I figured it was the ginger ale. I was allergic to ginger ale. Never once did this recovering gasoholic conceive that the problem might just be the gas. Christ. My cousin Bernie was the only member of my family who kept in touch. He'd come by my box and beg me to get help. 'Myron, Myron, what's a nice Jewish boy from the Bronx doing this for? To shame your parents?' He'd give me twenty bucks. I'd buy some panty hose, some lipstick, some vodka, and have plenty left over to keep my motor running for a week. . . ."

The feeling of warmth in the room was like an electric blanket. Faces all happy and rapt with attention — even sad-eyed mumblers were grooving to Myron's solo — heads nodding up and down with identification like those little plastic dogs in the rear windows of cars. It didn't take a rocket scientist to figure out that Myron's story was touching them all in some special way. The details were unique, but the emotions that drove him to the Gas

Chamber were universal. Feeling different — unloved, rejected, violated, terrorized, hopeless, helpless, despondent — and then the denial that a problem existed. That was a syndrome I knew only too well. The denial. When Michelle badgered me to get help and I'd tell her to get out of my face, that the problem was hers; when I got booted from the newspaper for one too many screwups; when I worked as a messenger and crashed the bike into a parked car or some faceless business suit crossing the street and I blamed it on traffic instead of the Lenny Bias-sized hit of crack I'd just sucked down; when I stole the kids' lunch money for a single vial of rock, then came back later that day and pawned their Nintendo box; when I ended up employed as a mopboy in a Times Square peepshow, swabbing semen from the floor for minimum wage, blaming society for my situation — when I did all that and still got sky-high, still kept stoking my head with cokedopeboozeweed and refused to admit that I was anything but normal, that was the hell of compulsion, the horror of obsession: that was denial. I'd become a dumb junkie, a blackout drinker, a loser.

I'd been on a mission, a long mission, and when I came to, the boys were sobbing and Michelle was yelling. I had no idea what I'd done, so I sat there and smoked a fat joint laced with crack and heroin, guzzled a warm flat beer, tried to block the awful noise of their lamentations out of my ears and piece together the preceding days. I couldn't remember. I was blank and filled with fear. As the substances played pinball in my brain, thrilling and chilling, zipping and zapping, the boys' moans got louder, more horrible, pounding at my weary brain like Muhammad Ali jabs and Joe Frazier hooks. Michelle's voice speared my head like a red-hot knitting needle inserted from ear to ear. I looked into their eyes and saw hate, misery, and fear. My heart ached. God help me, what had I done?

"My name is Ed," I said when Myron opened the meeting up to the floor, "and I'm a stupid stinking drug addict and alcoholic."

"Hi, Ed!"

"My wife is gone. She was right to leave. I was a mess. On the pipe 24/7. A dope-sniffing stemsucking crackerjack. The lowest form of life on the planet. I don't blame her for splitting. But I'm clean and sober now. Why can't it be a Hollywood ending? I don't understand. I miss my boys. I feel like taking some motherfucker by the throat and squeezing till his eyes pop right the fuck out."

"Listen, Ed." Myron spoke soothingly, like a mother, like a father, like a mother and father wrapped up in one. "Don't beat yourself up about it. You weren't in your right mind when you did all those things. The disease transformed you. You weren't responsible for your actions. Everyone in this room has done shit high we're not proud of." Heads bobbed. "I myself once siphoned gas from an ambulance on call. I stood there fifty feet away, gassing up on a Mobil martini, watching the paramedics wheel some poor bleeding fish out." He coughed nervously. "Ed, they couldn't start the vehicle. The guy maybe died. I don't know. I took off. A sober night doesn't go by I don't think about that man, pray for him, beg God's forgiveness. Look, by working The Program we learn to live with the past. Your wife is angry. With good reason. My own family, all except Cousin Bernie, took twenty-five years to forgive me; six of those years I was clean. You gotta give time time. Last month my youngest son was married, and I got invited. An Orthodox Jewish wedding, and they let me sit with the women. I wore a secondhand Halston and no one batted an eyelash. They forgave me, and now they accept me, for who I am, for what I was. You've been wandering in the woods for so long, you expect to find your way out in an instant? Give time time, Ed. Easy does it. Keep coming back. Hang in there. Take the toilet paper out of your ears and listen."

I listened. I'd been listening for hours. Rich people, poor people ("from Park Avenue to park benches," "from Yale to jail"), happy people, sad people ("from pink cloud to black shroud"). People who had conquered fear ("F-E-A-R, the active alcoholic's prime directive: Fuck Everything And Run"). People who wanted to kill, wanted to commit suicide, wanted to earn fortunes, or were content with nothing. People who lived with AIDS and wanted to die with dignity. People who loved, people whose hearts were breaking, who were jealous, angry, elated, deflated, constipated. Here was the human condition, every emotion and situation imaginable, and people were exulting in it. Living it sober. Sober! A word I once considered the filthiest in the English language. People living sober, people dying sober. It was beautiful, it was heartwarming, it was amazing — it was time for a drink.

Just one whiskey, I thought, as I filed with the penitents out of the church basement into the cold. Just one whiskey.

I felt a tap on the shoulder. Myron.

"It's the first one that gets you drunk."

"Mind your own business," I spat back. "The first will take the edge off. The sixth might get me drunk."

"Calm down, honey. Listen to me. You take that first drink you'll be back sucking a crackstem in no time. If you don't take that first drink you can't get loaded."

"Maybe I want to get loaded. It's not every day your wife kidnaps your kids and bolts. I deserve to get shit-faced. I want it. I need it."

"I don't think so." He circled my shoulders with his strong arm. "Why did you come to HDA?"

"Beats me."

"Drugs beat you. Booze beat you. Used you as a door-mat. Walked all over you and wiped streetshit onto your soul. Are you sick and tired of getting beat? Sick and tired of being sick and tired? You want to gain your family's respect? Maybe win them back?"

I nodded through the tears.

"Then come for coffee."

EIGHT cups of coffee later I had to piss like a racehorse. Myron sure could rap. Made a used car salesman seem downright shy, he was so enthusiastic about The Program. Peppering me with slogans and philosophy, he related the history of Hard Drugs Anonymous, its principles and practices, from the first historic meeting in Paynesville, Ohio, back in '34, between Big Jim Williams, the pro wrestler, and Farmer Rob Jones, a simple country boy who'd found he just couldn't get the crop in while zooted on morphine. The two alcoholic addicts had picked up their habits and their friendship in the hospital after being wounded in WWI, and almost two decades of shooting dope later (Farmer Rob was fond of claiming he was "the only fella in the Midwest who could find a needle in a haystack"), they desperately wanted to get clean. They'd tried every known remedy for addiction, taken all the cures, and still couldn't kick; but there, in that humble Ohio barn, midst a symphony of clucking chickens and oinking pigs, they realized that together — "We can do what I cannot" — through mutual support, one addict helping another, they could scrape the massive monkey off their backs and keep it away forever by just plain talking it to death. So as day stretched into evening, the air perfumed by the sweet country smells of hay and horse manure, they talked. Farmer Rob's wife, Lilly, fetched them coffee and apple pie, and they kept right on talking. They walked through fields of grain under star-studded skies, and talked, sharing their experience, strength, and hope; and by the time the sun nosed red over the horizon and the first rooster crowed, they'd given birth to the Twelve Steps of Hard Drugs Anonymous, the program of recovery that has flourished and spread over the years, mushroomed into a worldwide movement, been adopted by a wide variety of obsessive-compulsives, and provided a second chance, a bridge back to life, for countless millions of sufferers like myself and Myron, who'd managed to make a grade A mess out of things.

It wasn't easy sitting there at Leshko's, holding my water, while Myron, who had agreed to be my sponsor, jabbered away about Program ethics, tossing his bobbed black hair out of his eyes, sipping tea, delicate as a duchess, manicured pinkie finger poking out. My attention kept straying out the window to the street, to Tompkins Park, where the drug world flitted by like some grainy silent movie. Anxious addicts off to cop crack or heroin, then coming back a few minutes later with that buzzed look, that "don't worry be happy" jaunt to their step. Sure they were the lowest of the low, the slime of the earth, but they were damned happy slime, slime that felt no pain.

"I'm sorry." I turned to Myron. "What was that?"

"It's a simple program for complicated people. Remember what Big Jim said to Farmer Rob: 'Kiss. K-I-S-S. Keep It Simple, Stupid.' The best thing for a

newcomer is ninety meetings in ninety days. You'll have
a lot of feelings coming up, so don't stuff them. Talk
about them. Don't pick up a drink; pick up the phone.
Here are my numbers, at home and at work. Call anytime, about anything."

I was watching a skeletal whitegirl in a ratty old Chevy
right outside, hitting from a stem, could see her body
stiffen with a huge hit, then relax as she let the smoke
pour out her nose and cloud the car. Crackerjack heaven.
I was drooling.

"Ed, you have the disease. The AMA recognizes
addiction as a disease, a genetic disease. I'll bet a dollar
to a doughnut someone in your family suffers from it
too." I thought of my dead father, a real pig drinker,
pounding back the 7 and 7's like glasses of water. "The
only way to arrest your disease, one day at a time, is
working The Program. So keep coming back to meetings
and steer clear of people, places, and things that might
bring up urges."

Yeah, right, and move to Timbukfuckingtu.

"Sure, Myron. It was nice meeting you."

"Hang in there, Ed. Remember what Farmer Rob said
to Big Jim: 'The war is over and you lost.' Time to surrender. For The Program to work, you have to admit
you're powerless over all drugs and alcohol — that your
life is out of control. That's Step One."

His handshake was firm, his smile white. His little
breasts budded against the white silk blouse. And you
know, maybe if I had listened a little better, taken the
toilet paper out of my ears and really listened, if I hadn't
been so impressed with what a good-looking woman
Myron was for a man his age, maybe if I had drunk less

coffee or just simply used the restaurant's bathroom, or ducked around the corner into a bar and banged back a bunch of boilermakers, then maybe, just maybe, the next few days might have broken differently.

"Sure, Myron. And thanks," I said, trying to figure out his bra size.

I crossed into the park, past the rows of cardboard-box homes and tents known as Bushville, by blazing garbage-can fires where homeless men and women toasted their hands and guzzled beer, past dreadlocked Rastas hawking reefer, hissing "Cess! Cess!" like snakes, found a tree and took a steaming whiz, all the while thinking: Just one hit of crack, one delightful delicious lungful of the lip-numbing body-buzzing bubblegum-flavored cokesmoke. I could taste it, smell it, feel it. Then maybe a sniff of heroin, just an itty-bitty one, to get the complete okey-dokey, to forget that Michelle had abducted Mutt and Jeff (Matthew and Jeffrey) and was who-the-fuck-knows-where, probably sitting around her parents' home in Michigan, apple-cheeked Ma Kawalski weeping with re-lief she'd escaped madman Ed, while Pa K. showed the boys his gun collection and regaled them with bloody WWII stories. Myron had advised me not to call, to leave them be, repeating those phrases I'd already grown to hate: "Don't beat yourself up about it" and "Let go and let God." He was right. Sprinting full tilt into a brick wall would get me nowhere, only hurt, dazed, in further need of medication. To get better I had to consider Hard Drugs Anonymous my salvation, meetings my medicine, had to do ninety in ninety, talk about the pain, take that first baby step: admit I was powerless, that my life was out of control.

Not only was my life out of control, but so were my sneakers. Instead of splitting the park and cruising the few blocks down to Bowery and Houston, I was fast-stepping through the ruins of Alphabet City, what in the Pre-Gentrification Age people called Loisaida, heading for my favorite wholesale crack dealer. Goddammit, my feet were addicted.

I spoke into the intercom. "It's Ed." And the basement door buzzed open.

Flaco flopped in the torn leather recliner, so skinny he made Nancy Reagan look like an opera star on a diet of steroids and pizza, his unwashed black hair pulled back in a stylish ponytail. The big-screen TV blared "Life-styles of the Rich and Famous." Flaco slumped mesmerized, the bony face still as freeze-dried death, his crack-bright eyes glittering with the moneylust, on his lap a mean-ass gun. One hand held a crackstem, the other stroked his dog, a grinning all-white English bull terrier named Natasha, Spuds MacKenzie after a serious weightlifting program. She was chained to the radiator, her ball-peen hammer head oversized and elongated, with huge cruel fangs and prehistoric jaws. If Flaco didn't like you, she didn't hesitate to growl, bark, or strain at her chain. He fed her raw meat and junk food and was fond of bragging that she had once bit a Frenchman's dick in half.

"Yo, Flaco."

"Crack it up, homeboy. Wha'sup?" His eyes were glued to the tube. "Wha'sappenin'?"

"How's biz?" I asked, not caring, staring at the eight-inch crackstem growing from his burn-callused fingers, as Natasha nuzzled my crotch.

"Yo bro, what fo' dat bitch like you so much?"

"Maybe 'cause I don't feed her Yodels and Ding Dongs."

"Say, dude, you French?"

I kneeblocked Natasha's hard-probing slobberpuss. She sighed doggily and waddled back to the radiator.

"Sit you ass down, bro," he said, fixated on the television. "Look atta tits on dat broad. Ay, Mommy!"

The top-heavy starlet on-screen cavorted in Ty-D-Bol-blue Bermuda waters, toweled her tush, sipped a fruity rum drink, stuffed her white-toothed pouty-lipped kisser with dripping butter-dipped lobster.

"Oh, man!" moaned Flaco. "I lick da butta off huh tawpedoes and den I tear huh a new assho'."

He sure had a way with words. Housekeeping too. Natasha's shit piled stinking on urine-yellow newspapers. Walls and ceiling flaking, spotted with moving cockroaches. Sink overflowing with dishes. Ziploc bags open and full of crack, all in five-dollar vials with red caps, chunks of cokerock flashing bright like diamonds, gleaming white in the blue tubeglow like distant snowy blood-nippled mountains, surrounded by a green fluffy pile of cash.

My heart beat fast, my legs went boiled-spaghetti weak, my palms moist. A trickle of icy sweat raced down my ribs.

"Rock look good, huh Eddieboy?" He grinned. "Crack it up."

I swallowed a lump of nerves and grunted, tore my

gaze away and sat on the folding chair reserved for customers. The starlet was now riding a motor scooter down a dirt road shaded by palm trees, a road with plenty of potholes so her cleavage did the va-va-voom jiggle.

"Yo, bro, how dat peepshow job be treatin' you an' shit?"

"I got off that ride, man. You don't know how depressing it gets mopping spunk off the floor."

"Shit, Eddieboy, dat shit sound like fun an' shit. All dose wild chicks an' whatnot."

Yeah, like an all-expenses-paid vacation to Dante's Inferno.

"I've got an interview for a writing gig at the *Post* tomorrow," I lied.

"Booshit. You jos' a schemin' dreamin' crackaddick like da res' o' fockin' New York. O'ly way you make it onnada *Pos'* is you try ta rip me off and I gotsta shoot you white ass. Den you be page fockin' one an' shit." He laughed, displaying yellow rotten choppers splayed about his mouth like ancient bowling pins erupting in a strike.

"We friends or what?" I asked.

Flaco showed even more teeth.

"More like 'or what,' dude. Business is business. Crack it up, homeboy. How many you need?" He fingered the gun. Nasty-looking piece, a semiautomatic Glock pistol with silencer, lightweight plastic, seventeen shots, long and lethal and quiet as a butterfly's sneeze.

"Yo, Flaco my man, I'm a steady customer. Tonight I just happen to be tapped out. I'm looking to get turned on."

He found that hilarious. "You a chump, man. A one-man Comedy Store an' shit. You can smoke an' whatnot, bot I fockin' done los' all respeck an' shit. You pathetic."

He flicked his Bic, then ritually uttered the crackhead prayer of deliverance. "Beam me up, Scotty," he said, and drew orange flame into the crack-packed stem for a good twenty seconds, rotating the snap-crackle-popping tube, sucking hard on the blackening glass, cheeks scrunching, eyes bulging, scrawny chest inflating, temple veins pulsating, smoke trickling from his nose and mouth like a horror-movie skull.

He passed the hot stem and beamer, then exhaled a full cloud of roasted cokesmoke. The sweet bubblegum smell caressed my nostrils, tickled my tonsils. I held the tube, let it cool. The starlet was now doing aerobics, her heavy breasts bouncing in time to dance music.

"Whassamatta, crackhead? You don' wanna sock da Devil's Dick?"

I flicked the Bic. The torch shot six inches high, a neon invitation to hell. I put the stem to my lips, my quivering lips. I was shaking. Just one hit, what would that do? Lose Michelle forever? Fuckit, I thought. She was gone. Might as well get high, forget the pain of loss, smoke that shit and get a good fucking buzz. I made to hit on the stem (and here's where it gets weird — call it God, call it Freud, call it Fate), but it slipped from my jittery sweating fingers, fell to the floor with a crisp clink, the top inch snapping off.

"You clumsy fockin' drog begga!"

"Sorry," I mumbled.

"Sorry? You a sorry shit whiteboy. Get da fock ou' my house befo' I give you sorry dopefien' ass sumpin' you really be sorry bou'!"

I could feel the hot humiliated flush on my face. I

picked the stem up. The jagged edge gleamed bright in the TV's light. I touched it to my arm. A fat droplet of blood pearled on the skin and rolled warm and lazy down my wrist. I licked it and grinned. From the idiot box Robin Leach extolled the virtues of sun-kissed Bermuda, "where the natives are friendly and life is gentle."

"You a crazy mothafocka." Flaco waved the gun.

"Leave my mother out of it, crackerjack."

"Get the fock ou' or da dog be eatin' white meat fo' a week."

Natasha growled low from her throat.

"Fuck you and the banana boat you jumped off of," I said, standing. Then bingo! blackjack! gin! The answer bubbled forth clear as spring water, like a cartoon light bulb flash of inspiration, the solution to my problem with crack, the Final Solution: swift as Bruce Lee, I plunged the sharp seven inches of glass upward into Flaco's left eye hard as I could. A sick scream burbled from his throat, faded into a rattle, as his body did a spastic twitch and a shot of blood spurted through the hollow stem, splashed his surprised face.

He was good and dead before the dog could say "woof."

"Bull's-eye," I said, the sick weight lifting from my soul like night fog burned off by the dawn's early light. "Crack it up, homeboy."

"Nice dog," Myron said the next day, Monday, giving the bull terrier a leery look as we walked down lunchtime Broadway past Grace Church.

"Got her last night." I laughed at the memory of Natasha licking the blood off Flaco's face.

"You sure you're not manic-depressive? This is quite a mood swing. You're like the cat who ate the canary."

"More like the canary ate the cat."

"Yesterday you were miserable and heartbroken. Today you're Mr. Rogers."

" 'It's a beautiful day in the neighborhood,' " I sang. God, I felt happy, joyous and free, full of purpose and hope. "Myron, I love being clean and sober."

"Sounds like you're on the pink cloud. Whatever you're doing, just keep it up."

Myron looked so serious. In his fake-leopard coat, leopard-print boots, black stockings, and leopard beret, he was ravishing. Fit right in with all the downtown hipster types, the leather jackets and space age haircuts, skinheads, black kids with flattops and fades, hardcore kids with rainbow-colored Mohawks and spiketops flashing bright like exotic fishing lures.

"Here." I handed him a gift-wrapped package. "A token of thanks for saving me from demon rum."

"You shouldn't have," he said, ripping the wrapping. His eyes gaped. "Calvin Klein's Obsession! Ed! It's so expensive."

"Nothing but the best for my sponsor."

He spritzed his wrist, sniffed, and sighed.

"I love it," he said, then worry creased his face. "But can you afford it?"

"I came into some money."

Natasha scampered, so shiny and beautiful in her new black hair color (compliments of Miss Clairol), happy, smiling, puppylike, breathing the good cold air of winter after months shut up in Flaco's crackerjack hellhole.

"You really like my dog?"

"No offense, Ed, but she's a fucking land shark."

"I took her from a crack dealer. He kept her chained up and fed her Twinkies. I liberated her." Natasha certainly had adjusted well to the change in ownership.

"You got high?"

"Hell no. I'm through with that sucker action. I'm clean and serene."

"You think I was born yesterday?"

"Myron, I'm telling the truth. As you said last night, this is a program of rigorous honesty."

"You went to a crack dealer's house and you didn't get high? Ed, you can't bullshit a bullshitter."

"I wanted to get high — "

"Ah, the truth comes out. As Big Jim said, 'Drop by a barbershop, end up with a haircut.' That's why you gave me the perfume. Guilty conscience."

"I swear I didn't get high. Last night I killed a guy."

Myron's eyes bugged in disbelief. "You got it. I waxed him but good. Dusted the motherfucker. He was a total slime. He tried to victimize me. I ain't no vic. So I took his life. Then I took his dog, his cash, his gun, his ammunition. Today I paid my rent and phone bill, and Jesus, I haven't felt this good in years. And I didn't smoke crack."

We walked along in silence. Myron shook his head.

"Ed, I don't know what to say."

"How about, 'Don't beat yourself up about it'?"

"Frankly, young man, I don't believe your crazy story. Are you a compulsive liar? As your sponsor, I suggest you go to a lot of meetings and take the toilet paper out of your ears and put it in your mouth. Step Two tells us that a power greater than ourselves can restore our sanity. You're gonna have to get in touch with your Higher Power, Ed."

I was a little miffed that he had me tabbed as a nutcase. I mean, here he was pushing fifty-five, wearing teeny-bopper outfits. Well, maybe it was safer that way.

"Ed, you're a sick young man. Don't be so defiant. As Big Jim said, 'Reliance, not defiance.' Have faith. Trust the process. Trust your Higher Power. Stay clean and pray."

"I haven't prayed since I was a kid."

"Start praying. But not in a selfish manner. Ask God to show you the way. Say, 'Thy will be done.' "

"Thy will be done," I said. "Hey, that feels pretty good."

"Of course it does. Turning your will and life over to the care of God is Step Three. The beginning of a new freedom."

"Speaking of free, Myron, can I buy you lunch?"

"Thanks, but I need to get back to the office. A woman's work is never done."

"You saving up for that operation?"

"God willing," he said, looking skyward. Then he giggled. "A girl's gotta do what a girl's gotta do."

"Myron, the Obsession smells great on you."

"I'll pray for you, Ed."

"Pray for Natasha too."

I SAT in Washington Square Park, deserted in the cold but for the pigeons and a few crack dealers pacing the perimeter. I drank coffee, watched Natasha chomp a hot slice of pizza, tomatoed mozzarella steaming and stretching, snapping and slapping her muzzle.

I felt as giddy and goofy as a kid hunched over a paper bag huffing model airplane glue, feeling the sweet dizzy of the childhood buzz. I'd get my wife and kids back, and we'd be a nice normal family with a nice normal dog. Just had to give time time, stay away from that first drug or drink, not beat myself up about it all. Beat myself up? I deserved a Congressional Medal of Honor for wiping out that slimebucket Flaco. I was a soldier in the President's war on drugs.

One week since I'd checked into detox. Over twenty years abusing drugs, par for the course for m-m-m-m-my generation. The detox staff at the hospital had tried to get me to check into a twenty-eight day rehab. They'd even called the Veterans Administration to set it up. I told them, "Fuck that noise. I've got a family to take care of, a wife who's working as a waitress and two food-vacuum kids." They told me I needed time away from the streets, that I was a "ticking time bomb." I laughed and said I could stay straight whatever came up. I was a grown man. Thirty-three years old, six feet tall, a hundred and sixty pounds — same as when I joined the navy fifteen years back (all the walking and not-eating and nerves of the lowlife highlife kept me lean and mean) — and my blond hair was still crew-cut. I was tough. No one could make me get high except me.

The night before, Myron had explained the "elevator concept" of the disease: "You can get off on any floor, or you can go on down to the grease pit." Well, baby, I was born in the grease pit.

I was a teenage drugfiend, always on the hunt for injectables — coke, dope, and speed. I just about lived in shooting galleries, and my expertise with the spike made me very popular. I started on that scene following my old man's pistol-sucking sayonara (he couldn't face a lingering death from alcohol-induced pancreatic cancer and a liver crisp as bacon) and bagged it after I got into a scrape and the juvenile authorities shipped me upstate to a long-term boot camp rehab/reform school, where they shaved my head, sat me in a corner wearing a dunce cap and a sign around my neck that read: I AM A WORTH-LESS PIECE OF SHIT GARBAGEHEAD. The only positive by-product of that hellhole: I swore off needles and powders. Released, age eighteen, I joined the navy. My time in the service was a two-year worldwide whirl of hookers, hash-ish, and international barfights. On board ship I smoked hash and consumed the ship's library, the Reader's Digest condensed classics, as many as I could. The last thing I wanted to be was a lifer in the navy or a garbageman like my father. Back in New York, after a series of dead-end stupid-dick gigs, I got a copyboy job at a newspaper, met Michelle, and we had some beautiful years. After the boys were born I became a reporter, and except for pot and beer I was a good boy.

But then along came Scotty, and I signed up for a five-year mission to explore strange new worlds. In order to balance the crack I snorted heroin or drank whiskey, and the habits had snowballed, until they avalanched my life. That winter had been the worst. Smoking and sniffing and drinking until my family was completely alienated. I didn't give a shit. I'd do anything for the next hit. I even sold the fancy sneakers Michelle gave me as a Christmas present from money she'd earned as a waitress, traded them for two vials of jumbo, and walked home barefoot in the snow, no money for groceries, one of Scotty's mutants. At the peepshow I'd stare into a grungy bucket full of mopwater and sperm, looking in the sad muddy swirl for clues as to what had happened. All I knew was the craving for crack. I was in the grease pit. Myron had quoted Farmer Rob: "The disease of addiction attacks and destroys on four levels, the physical, the emotional, the mental, and the spiritual." Bingo! I'd become spiritually dead, physically numb, mentally dumb, and emotionally constipated.

My earliest memories are of watching black-and-white television through the bars of my crib, seeing good-guy gunslingers waste evil Old West motherfuckers, listening to my father scream at my mother.

Pop, a two-fisted boozer, worked for the NYC Sanitation Department. When I was five or six and his army buddies were over, he'd let me drink beer. Ma objected, but shut up pronto when he shot her one of his chilling looks. I didn't much care for the taste, but I loved the warm glow. Pop was consumed by resentment, angry that his promising baseball career had been wrecked by WWII and "those fucking Japs." (He'd been a POW, badly treated, and a poorly set shattered tibia resulted in one leg's being shorter than the other.) He'd come home from work drunk, stinking of garbage and Clancy's Bar, complain about everything — dinner, hippies, the neighborhood. He'd chuck me under the chin with a big rough hand, limp across the living room, collapse in his chair, watch TV, and when Ma came near to check if he was passed out — boom! — he'd smack her before she could dart away. He never remembered hitting her, but for days after, the sight of her eggplant-purple bruises and split lips would sober him up, and we'd be a family: go on picnics or to a ballgame or the movies. In general he was an asshole. Hated to see me cry. I learned to hide my feelings. When he was drinking, it was terrible. One time Ma was visiting her dying father and Pop went on a bender, kept me chained naked to the radiator for two days, feeding me bread and water, making me do my duty in a bucket, punching me, kicking me, calling me a dirty little Jap, and. . . .

He pushed me to be a scholar and an athlete, forbade me to go to church with Catholic Ma, and insisted I keep my hair short. I dreamed of becoming a hippie, to get some of the drugs and free love advertised by the counterculture. I discovered reefer, acid, and glue sniffing in sixth grade and never turned back. For more kicks I became a ripoff. Just petty stuff, but like superslick jewel thief Alexander Monday from TV, it became a lifestyle. A piece of bubblegum was a diamond, a candy bar solid gold. Porno magazines were classified documents. Ma found my collection but, fearing the old man's vengeance, never ratted. So I went at it even harder. I stole and stole and ate that sugary crap until my teeth were rotting with cavities and I had to spend every Friday for a year in the dentist's chair, scrambled on laughing gas. I looked forward to Fridays.

Pop's religion was pro sports, but he loved the nightly news, the footage from Vietnam. I rooted for the Vietcong. I identified with him, the little guy. Every Christmas and birthday, Pop gave me a G.I. Joe doll, and I would play Charlie. I went to Chinatown and stole a straw coolie hat. I'd tape my eyelids to appear Oriental, put on the hat, then go to work on Joe: saw off limbs, torture him with burning cigarettes as he remained stoic during intense questioning, dip his hands and feet in acid from my chemistry set, smack his head repeatedly with a hammer, soak his clothes with lighter fluid, torch him, hang his burning body out the window to swing for the downstairs neighbors, reel him in, decapitate him, douse and ignite him again, chuck him flaming out my fifteenth-floor window, watch him plummet screamless in a beautiful orange arc, slicing the New York night skyline with the greatest of ease, silent to the last, not even a whimper, landing on the street below, burning, skin molten and bubbling, spewing black smoke, sidestepped and stared at by uncaring citizens.

Grandpa died, left Ma ten grand, and in possibly the only assertive act of her life, to keep Pop from drinking the money dry, she insisted on sending me to prep school.

* * *

There is a green hill far, far away, beyond the city grime, where bad little boys are sent to spare their parents sleepless nights and trips to the police station.

St. Dismas boasted a splendid green campus, where heavy drinking and drugging were the norm.

I showed up with a trunkful of stolen hardcore porno and set up shop, loaning the magazines in exchange for drugs. Monster jocks and four-eyed bookworms alike showered me with respect and reefer. I amassed a great fortune in weed: Thai sticks, Mongolian Mindfuck, Acapulco and Colombian Gold, Panama Red, Jamaican, hash, hash oil — smoke that made the body shiver, the upper lip sweat, the brain sizzle, the eyes go blood red and basset hound droopy.

Soon a few of the younger teachers were customers, paying cash. What a sweet setup! Life was fun. Once, the whole freshman class congregated in the woods to watch the gymnastic Mal Fox blow himself to orgasm. Autumn zoomed by in a haze of reefer and rainbow foliage, parties in the woods with guys named Chipper, Kip, Buzz, and Chauncey. The long winter evenings we'd ski cross-country under star-plastered skies, stopping to nip from flasks and smoke delicious joints. We'd drop acid and skate the pond for hours on black ice so thick and clear you could see fish all blocked up for winter, the moon flashing bright off skateblades, leaving trails, the LSD juicing our souls, making our bodies feel weightless. We'd drink bourbon or rum for a buck a shot out at Armin's Cabin, an old shack beyond Opiated Rock. Or we'd sit on logs, passing pipes like Indians of old, chewing the fat, shooting the shit, lying about girls. Those were good nights.

Not for long. My library got busted, my literature confiscated. I was put on probation and sent to the teacher who doubled as campus shrink, Rock Romaine. Rock let me smoke cigarettes in our sessions. "Why do you feel different from the other boys?" he'd ask. "Because my name's not Chip or Lawrence or Barnaby. I come from the city. From a shitty neighborhood. I'm not a WASP. I don't own a convertible or a stereo, don't have a girlfriend named Muffy or Missy." "Do you hate yourself?" He'd offer a cig. "No," I'd say and light up. "Why do you hate yourself?" "I don't hate myself." "Then why this need for attention?"

I didn't fit in. My family didn't have money, hadn't come over on the *Mayflower*. I didn't wear the right clothes, speak like they did. After my porn biz went belly-up, they turned on me, treated me as an outsider. I wasn't considered useful or nice any longer. I didn't know the limits. The guys pegged me as a leech. When I entered smoking rooms, conversations jerked to mumbles. Former get-high buddies would square their jaws, avoid my eyes, ignore my greetings.

Over spring break I begged my parents to let me stay home. No way. Poor folk want their money's worth.

When I got back to campus I found a condom full of blood on my door handle. I pulled it off and it splattered, soaking my old canvas Keds. (Later I learned they'd sacrificed a woodchuck for the occasion.) Outside, the snows had melted and the crocuses were poking their pretty yellow heads out of the rich New England soil, but inside,

I felt worthless. Less than human. I walked around in bloody sneakers. The message was clear: leech.

They treated me like a leper with bad breath and dandruff, jumped me in the woods, beat the shit out of me, sent me hate mail. I quote from bitter memory: "Dingleberry, dingleberry, you are shit caked in an ass so hairy."

I took my last hidden smut mag to the woods and set it aflame. As the final gigantic set of breasts in a pictorial titled "Suburban Milk Sluts in Heat" crisped to ash, I vowed to get even.

I reverted to Alexander Monday form and ripped off drugs, radios, cookies, clothes, and record albums. I buried the booty in a pine grove deep in the woods. Late at night I'd lie in bed and smoke joints, watch a pop-up TV that I'd permanently borrowed from an insect-repellent-company heir who was blowing his Latin teacher so he could make A's and get into Harvard. I slept little and spoke rarely. Rock Romaine was worried.

Then one day close to summer, as birds twittered and squirrels scampered, as sunlight shafted through the pines, as I smoked a fat joint and proudly surveyed the pitful of rusting radios, rain-soaked clothes, and warped records, I got nailed.

Two whooping seniors broke from the trees and pinned me to the pine needle carpet.

"What have we here?" asked the dashing blond lacrosse star and up-and-coming socialite Hunter Lodge, Jr.

"The Leech is the fucking thief," stated the flowing-maned Bennett Cottingham VI.

They whacked me around, stripped me naked, lashed me to a tree with cords ripped from radios, stuffed my mouth with a moldy hundred-percent-cotton Brooks Brothers sock, then split.

Mosquitoes congregated and lunched on my bloody face. Flies tickled my lips. I strained to get loose, but the cords only dug deeper. Birds sang. Deer hopped by, pausing with noses all aquiver to stare at the white form stuck to a tree. Chipmunks eyed my nuts. Sock in mouth, I couldn't yell. The sun lowered to the west. The air grew cooler and the nightshift skeeters came on duty. All I could think was: God, if you get me out of this I'll never get high again.

A hundred cruel faces stood before the tree.

"Lynch the Leech!"

A cheer cascaded from the mass. I was scared shitless. They built a fire, though the moon was fat and bright, and the boys, many of them man-sized, hulked, smoked reefers and cigarettes, cigars and pipes, guzzled beers, tippled bottles.

Hunter Lodge, Jr., wore Day-Glo-pink tights, a black bow tie on bare chest, an Abe Lincoln stovepipe hat, hiking boots, and granny glasses. He was drunk as a motherfucker.

"Leech," he slurred, "I am your persecutor."

A high-pitched voice piped up, "I'm your defense attorney." It was Waldo Wentworth, the pot dealer.

Bennett Cottingham VI chimed in, "And I'm your judge, asshole." He pointed at the human piranhas by the blazing fire. "These handsome gentlemen are your jury."

Fear tightened my scrotum.

"Grolsch!" cried Cottingham, invoking the name of the most popular beer on campus.

"Grolsch!" echoed the many.

"Before we get this show on the road, as judge of the St. Dismas Kangaroo Court, tradition requires that I ask if there are any announcements."

"Grolsch!" yelped Waldo. "I'd like to alert the jury that I'm selling dynamite Mexican weed, light fluffy green, kickass, thirty bucks an ounce. Fat bags, great weed. Come and get it."

"Order in the court." Bennett Cottingham VI was angry. My defense attorney was doing brisk business. "Waldo's ounces are only twenty-six grams, and I happen to have exotic Temple Ball hash made by Zen monks in a monastery in Tibet that will blow Waldo's cheap shit down the toilet. Six bucks a gram, five for twenty-five."

Transactions. Fire crackling, beer cans popping, matches flaring, Zippo lighters clicking open and shut, tokes being coughed, and the otherworldly drone of crickets.

"According to tradition" — Cottingham spoke in his upper-crust Boston accent — "everyone gets a slap and a spit."

They banged my face and spit on my body. Pain and humiliation. My ears rang.

"What's that you say?" Cottingham pulled the sock.

"Fuck you," I croaked.

"Fighting spirit. Very admirable, Leech." He cocked his fist and slammed my mouth. Yes, it hurt, and I tasted blood.

"Grolsch, is the prosecutor ready to commence?"

Hunter Lodge, Jr., blew out his toke, swigged a brew, primped his tie. "Ready."

"C'mon, guys," I begged. "Lay off. I'm sorry."

"Sorry?" screamed Lodge. "You stole my favorite alligator shirt!"

"Took an ounce of pot from me!"

"My Top-Siders."

"My sister's Laura Nyro record."

"My oatmeal cookies."

"Thief!"

"Leech!"

"Slime!"

"Grolsch!"

"I didn't mean to hurt anyone."

Waldo stepped forward. At least someone was on my side.

"Gents, I have two bags of weed left. Full ounces. The price is twenty-five. . . . Look, sure the Leech is guilty, but he's just a child. A space cadet. His family is poor. I say suspended sentence and let's party. Fat bags, great weed, free rolling papers."

"He's guilty!" Hunter Lodge, Jr., was not to be denied. "He's a ripoff! Sacred radios, L. L. Bean clothing, pot, and the cookies our dear mothers' maids baked for us with love and care! He's white trash! Convict the bastard."

"Please," I implored them. "Can't we just forget this ever happened? I'll never do it again."

"A Lodge never forgets."

"You have my word of honor." I was desperate.

"The word of a leech?" Lodge pranced in the firelight,

pink tights glowing. "You know what I think of that?"

"I didn't know Neanderthals could think."

Hunter Lodge, Jr., approached, lowered his tights, and, oh Jesus, took a leak. I turned my head. The hot stinking stream flowed over me, soaked me with humiliation.

"Leech." He laughed maliciously. "You've finally succeeded in pissing me off."

"Grolsch!" they cheered. I felt like crying.

Bennett Cottingham VI looked at his Rolex. "Time is short, jury. What's the verdict?"

"Guilty!" they screamed as one.

"The sentence?"

Lodge raised his hand. "Tradition calls for a nutty."

"Nutty! Nutty! Nutty!" they chanted.

"A nutty?" Hunter Lodge, Jr., smiled shyly, like a wallflower being asked to dance.

"Grolsch!" came the harsh roar.

"Please don't," I begged, choking on mucus, tears shooting from my eyes. Jesus, I hated them.

Hunter Lodge, Jr., approached, burped, arranged his tights.

"Not a nutty, please, not that."

"It's a St. Dismas tradition. Ugly worthless trash like you have been nuttied here for a hundred years. Why, in my granddaddy's time —"

"Nutty! Nutty!" they chanted.

My heart raced. I had trouble breathing. The fire crackled and sparked. Faces leered, voices cheered.

Hunter Lodge, Jr., gripped my right testicle and commenced to squeeze.

Horrible intense pain. Blinding, awful pain. I

screamed at the pain, swallowed the puke that filled my throat, screamed and screamed and screamed as they counted and cheered, counted and laughed. At twenty, my bowels opened up, and that's the last I remember.

When I awoke, the moon was high in the black starry sky. Rock Romaine was snipping my bonds with wire cutters. Someone had snitched. "Jesus!" he said. "The bastards." I was beaten, bug-bit, stinking, stiff, bloody, numb, in shock. Romaine half carried me back to campus, washed me, put me to bed under blankets on his couch. In the morning he brought me coffee spiked with whiskey, lit two smokes, handed one to me, and asked, "What the hell happened out there?"

And all I could say was, "Grolsch."

" . . . AND so it came to pass— one mo' time — I lost everything. Everything. I spent fifteen months sucking shit through a sock in a mental hospital with guys that smoked cigarettes out of their noses and gave each other split pea soup shampoos. My only pleasure was Ping-Pong. I was champion of the bin. After being diagnosed as an incurable manic-depressive alcoholic with psychotic tendencies and a great spin serve, I was discharged from the flight deck with a clean bill of health. I was ready for more punishment. I thought I could be a social drinker and a social intravenous coke user. Like Farmer Rob says, 'Stinking thinking leads to serious drinking.' And boy, did I ever drink. I bullshitted my way into a great job on Madison Avenue, so I had plenty of dough to kill myself with. As Big Jim said, 'Money is a mood changer.' Wasn't long before I was back to shooting coke and drinking vodka alone in my apartment. I was Billy B., the great I AM. Guess what? I was just a lonely sick fuck dreaming behind drawn shades. Wearing a mask. I figured I was cured. Hey, I wasn't hearing voices. It got so I never left the crib. I ordered out for coke and booze and the occasional wonton soup — that's all I could keep down. Paranoid? I hid in the closet when the phone rang, convinced the cops were after me. I lived in fear. I was spooked by my own shadow. Sucking shit through a sock. So yet again I lost everything. Ended up on the streets, a raving fucking bum, sleeping on subways, collecting cans, begging change for wine. That two years was one long blackout. I came out of it right here in this room, and I've been coming back ever since. You people fed me, gave me clothes, let me sleep on your couches. You said, 'Let us love you till you can love yourself.' I hated myself. I had a liver the size of a grapefruit. A bleeding ulcer. Gastritis. And acne. I had more zits than there are stars in the sky. I detoxed through my skin. Yet still you loved me. Loved me when I couldn't love myself. You told me it would get better, if only I believed in God, in the fellowship of HDA. You told me to have faith. To not stuff my feelings. At first I couldn't see a God Almighty, so I translated G-O-D down to Group Of Druggies, and it worked, it truly worked. I am a miracle. I used to be a nasty asshole sucking shit through a sock, and now I'm a human being with feelings. I live very simply and work with quadriplegics. I avoid slippery people and slippery places, because I may still have another binge in me but I don't believe I have another recovery. Most of the time I'm happy. Not every day. Sometimes I don't want to feel what I'm feeling, but I don't self-medicate: I go through whatever it is that's bothering me, and I talk about it. You all help me, and if I can, I help you. That's what it's all about. One addict helping another. I don't drink or drug, and I come to meetings to arrest my disease, one day at a time. Sobriety is a wonderful journey. If I do what I need to do today,

God takes care of tomorrow. If you have doubts, please don't go back out there. Take my word, it's the heart of fucking darkness. Don't leave five minutes before the miracle. I love you all and thank you for my recovery."

Thunderous applause greeted the pockmarked boozer's finale. They passed the basket and asked who had an anniversary or under ninety days.

"My name's Mohammed," spaketh a dark-skinned man. "I'm an addict, and by the will of Allah I have fifty-eight days." Everyone clapped.

"My name is Francine," murmured a Chinese woman in a fur coat. "I'm an alcoholic and cocaine addict, and I have eleven days."

"My name is Arnold." This from a chubby whiteboy with blond hair and a Midwest accent. "By the grace of God and this Fellowship, I got four days off crack and dope."

"My name is Ed, and I'm a stupid stinking drug addict and alcoholic. Including detox, this is day seven." Hey, they were cheering for me! It felt nice. I pet Natasha's funny sharkhead.

"My name's Luis, alcohol and drugs, and I got eighty-nine days."

"Loo! Loo! Loo!" barked the crowd.

Then they did the anniversaries of a year or more and I could see the serenity beaming on the faces.

"We'll go to a show of hands."

"My name is Rachel," announced the cover-girl type who'd welcomed me so warmly after my first meeting, "and I'm a drug addict and alcoholic."

"Hi, Rachel!"

Black ringlets of hair framed a statue-perfect face so

heartbreakingly lovely as to shame Greta Garbo to the plastic surgeon, flowed down her slim smooth neck, cascaded in coils down her back, tickled magnificent breasts that pressed against her white T-shirt, breasts that'd make the snowy Himalayas melt green with envy. She couldn't have been older than twenty-two.

"I've got about three years clean time," she said. "And the longer I stay away from my drugs of choice, cocaine and alcohol, the more I act out in other ways. I've been eating like a small elephant." It didn't show. Her jean-sheathed legs were slim and curvaceous, with fine lines that would shame Helen of Troy to the health club. "I guess you might say I'm stuffing my feelings. Since I broke up with my boyfriend, my ex-significant other, I've been obsessing about sex." The men in the room — and more than a few of the women — eyed her hungrily, like a tribe of cannibals after a six-month onion-and-mud fast. "My ex is relapsing. The disease of addiction has him by the balls. I kicked him out of our apartment, and even though he brutalized me and I hate him, I miss the sex. Does that make me a sex addict? Like that guy who says he's a stupid stinking drug addict, am I a sleazy slimy sex addict? I want more more more more more more more more." She paused. "And then I'd like some more. Not just sex either. I want more food, more fun, more acting jobs, more friends. I've really got to be careful. That's the way I was with cocaine. When I was high, I underwent a personality change. Hey, I even acted under the stage name Jacqueline Hyde. I'd do anything for more. My nose was finished — deviated septum. I hated needles, had a bronchial infection in my lungs and couldn't smoke free-base — crack, free-base: really they're the same damn thing. But guess what? I had to have more coke. I'd hang upside down from inversion boots and take a cocaine and Perrier enema. Talk about catching a buzz! With enemas like that, who needs friends?"

The crowd groaned at the joke.

"Talk about keeping the memory of your bottom green! Every time I see a Perrier bottle, I remember the horror. And food! I don't like talking about it, but when I was a kid I couldn't stop eating, binging out on food. I grew up in an orphanage. Every time I got adopted, the foster parents would be so happy to have this cute little girl. But after a month max, binging and purging, binging and purging, once they figured out the grocery bills, they'd send me back. And now it's the sex. You know what Big Jim said: 'Put some gratitude in your attitude.' Well, I am grateful, but that doesn't take care of my sex drive. I know I should be looking to God for serenity, but you ever try having sex with God? As Farmer Rob said, 'God can move mountains, but it pays to bring along a shovel.' Where's my shovel?"

"Thank you, Rachel," said Billy B., nodding. "You said the word 'should.' You 'should' be looking to God. I have a sign in my bathroom, a quote from Farmer Rob: 'Today I will not should on myself.' God can move mountains, but he won't unless we help. That's the 'shovel,' the willingness to participate in the miracle."

Rachel smiled sweetly. It was hard to imagine she'd ever been a slut, let alone a free-base freak, yet there it was, she'd copped to it. It was like hearing Shirley

Temple fess up to turning pre-teen tricks on the back lots of Hollywood, licking Jack Warner's kosher wiener instead of a candy cane. My heart went out to her.

"Look." Billy B. pounded his message home. "Fighting God's will is like sucking shit through a sock. Pray for guidance. And as Big Jim said, 'There's a whole lot of power in just being powerless.' And if you don't believe yet, fake it till you make it."

I wanted off drugs, sure, but the Hallelujah Bandwagon wasn't exactly my idea of a speedy getaway car. God restoring us to sanity, God moving mountains, God buying us ice cream cones and granting us serenity, God removing the obsession to get high. God, I was sick of hearing about God.

The guy next to me, a stringbean whiteboy with a surfer's tan and washed-out green eyes, had his arm raised. Billy B. pointed his way.

"My name is Chester Z. and I'm, like, a drug fanatic."

"Hi, Chester!"

"Like I'm visiting from California, and this is a bitchin' meeting. Very spiritual, you know. But this dude sitting next to me groans every time someone says the G word. As Big Jim said, 'This is a program of attraction, not promotion.' And I wouldn't like want him to think HDA is a cult or a religion or something. When they say God, Ed, they mean God as you understand him or her. Whatever works for you. God. Goddess. Toaster oven. Up to you. Me? I use Good Orderly Direction and Group Of Druggies, 'cause I find the healing powers of the collective unconscious in these rooms to be very radical. I get a sense of, you know, universal harmony when I come to HDA meetings. Ed, you're a new-

comer." He grinned, showing me his gapped teeth.
"You're the most important person here. Just relax and
dig the sense of peace, the flow. If Chester Z. can get
The Program, anyone can. I drank and drugged since I
was six. Weed, speed, glue, acid, mushrooms, Carbona
carpet cleaner, coke, dope, liquor, pills, crack, you name
it. If it got you high I did it. But you know what got me
clean and sober? What brought me to my knees? It was
frogs, man. That's right, frogs."

Oh shit, another lunatic.

"I took to licking frogs. Cane toads. Like their skin
secretes a chemical that gets you real high. They're big,
you know, the size of a Frisbee, and you can only find
them in the desert. I was so broke I took to hitching into
Death Valley to lick frogs; but then I got sunstroke and
could only go out at night. So I broke into the reptile
room at the San Diego Zoo, and that's where I got busted,
like down on my knees, licking a big slimy frog. I pulled
a year, and it was in the joint, doing my bit, that I got
the message of Hard Drugs Anonymous. I finally licked
my drug problem, and I've been like coming back ever
since. Big Jim said, 'You're either walking toward a buzz
or away.' Like I've got my Nikes on and I'm sprinting
away, man. You know, one day at a time I don't lick that
first frog. If I need to keep the memory green, I just turn
on 'The Muppets' and watch Kermit. Today the only
time I like get down on my knees is when I pray."

"My name's Jerome, and I'm a crack addict."

"Hi, Jerome!"

"Thanks for kicking it, man." He was a mocha-
skinned man in a three-piece suit, with a briefcase on his
lap. "When I bottomed out, the world was a cold cruel

motherfucker. I couldn't get off the pipe. I tried to quit a thousand times, but it just wasn't God's time. That glass dick was my pacifier. I smoked crack morning, noon, and night. Scotty was my boyfriend, dig? And I'm a ladies' man. I stuffed my feelings with cocaine. Bet, the last time I got high I was so beamed up, I took this huge motherfuckin' hit and sat on the goddamn stem. It broke, burnt my ass, and, check it out, sliced it so bad I had to make a run to the hospital. Yo, from there to detox and then to rehab. Check it out, they saved my ass. Like I was toxic, baby! I came in on the Third Step, turned my will and my life over to the care of God, and it was like walking blindfolded in outer space. I had to trust the process. Had to let go and let God. Today I show up for life. I wear my sobriety like silk drawers. I work a good solid HDA Program and I live by those Twelve Steps. On a daily basis I arrest my disease. I make good money, but bet, it won't mean jackshit if I don't stay clean. Anytime I forget how bad it was, I look at my butt and see the scars from when I hit my bottom. Thanks for listening, and keep coming back. It works if you work it. I thank God for that broken crackstem."

"That's right, my man, no more sucking shit through a sock."

"My name is Agatha." A tiny white-haired old lady. "I'm a heroin addict and alcoholic."

"Hi, Agatha!" She waved like a grandmother on a game show.

"I'm eighty-eight years old," stated the wrinkled lady. "And I shot morphine and drank for over sixty years. I identify with wearing a mask. At the end I was Agatha P., on the outside a sweet little old grandma, but underneath I was a monster. I'd cheat at bridge, con my friends for their Social Security checks, shoplift from the supermarket. You know what it feels like having three or four cold steaks down your bloomers? Brrrr." She shuddered. "I used to beg money from my children. Once, I even filched ninety-four cents from my youngest grandkid's piggy bank. I needed a beer that bad. I was spiritually dead. Now I pray. When I first came around I called God Fred. I was at a meeting, and a fellow said, 'Agatha, the reason you're so miserable is that you don't call God by his proper name. God's name is Harold. Our father who art in heaven, Harold be thy name.' Now that I pray to Harold, all my needs are met. I have no problems, and I haven't had a gin rickey or a shot of dope in seven years. And as you're so fond of saying, Billy B., I don't have to suck shit through a sock anymore."

"My name is Ed," I said when Billy B. picked me, "and I'm a stupid stinking drug addict and alcoholic."

"Hi, Ed!"

"Last night I wanted to get high. Despite all the love I felt in this room, I wanted the zap."

The room seemed hot and small. I felt the probing eyes on me. Where's that fucking Myron? He's not here. There's Rachel. She's got sympathy to burn. She's an angel.

"But I didn't do any drugs." I felt sweat bubbling on my forehead. "I don't know how to deal with all the shit I'm feeling. I really miss my wife, the sorry-ass bitch. Sure the marriage was sour, but I thought getting clean would save it. My sponsor says to be patient, to give time time. I'd like to give time a boot in the ass. It's like I'm on a roller coaster. One minute up, next minute down.

I want my family back so bad, but if I get high I'll lose them forever. Part of me wants to get blitzed, I mean really fucking ossified. I deserve that."

"Sounds like you want to beat yourself up about it, Ed," said Billy B. "As Farmer Rob said, 'When the heart wails for what it has lost, the soul laughs for what it has found.' You may not know it now, but being clean and sober is a new freedom, a beautiful liberation from the tyranny of drugs. Easy does it. You no longer have to suck shit through a sock."

Billy B. smiled. I smiled back. Rachel smiled. I smiled back. I felt better for having shared, I really did. Maybe I wasn't such a bad person.

"My name is Frank, and I'm a fuckin' drug addict and alcoholic."

"Hi, Frank." A lukewarm greeting. And I knew why. I'd seen him the night before, but he hadn't really registered. He had some of the coldest eyes I'd ever seen. A square unshaved jaw. As a reporter you get to know faces and types, and as a junkie you learn to recognize the Franks of the world, from two blocks off. There was no mistaking the mug on this duck. He was a cop. Hundred-percent all-American power-fed cop. And just looking at him did something unpleasant to my stomach.

"I'm eight months fuckin' sober, and it ain't fuckin' easy. First the fuckin' rehab and the divorce, and now these crazy fuckin' meetin's. And even though I like bein' clean and fuckin' sober, I don't fuckin' feel comfortable. You grateful crazy shitbirds think just 'cause I'm a cop you can't fuckin' trust me. You think I was planted here to fuckin' spy on you? Gimme a fuckin' break. What are you, paranoid? I was caught shootin' two bags of the devil's dandruff in the fuckin' precinct men's room by a born again fuckin' hard-on captain. When I was active I needed a drink or a drug every morning just to face the fuckin' day. If that don't make me an addict, fuck you. So now I'm on fuckin' suspension. I live in a fuckin' welfare hotel, and I gotta buy the fuckin' *Post* just to keep up with the murder scene. Today I read where a fuckin' scumbag got it with a stem in the eye, dead as a stale fuckin' doughnut. How's that for poetic fuckin' justice! Let the fuckin' bacteria wipe each other out."

I wanted to laugh. He was right.

"Saves the courts time. Saves the taxpayers moolah. Makes the city safer. But some fuckin' days I feel like shootin' a few bags or havin' a nice game of one-on-one with Jack fuckin' Daniel's. Who says cops don't have feelin's? I'm a sensitive fuckin' guy. Just wish I had some fuckin' friends. Thanks."

"Easy does it, Frank." Billy B. soothed the blue-jawed cop with the long black hair. "Drinking or shooting dope won't make the pain go away; it'll just hide it for a while. Your disease wants you six feet under, sucking shit through a sock. Don't listen to it. Come with me for coffee after the meeting. We'll talk." Billy B. was reaching out, helping another sufferer. What a great program! It works. It truly works! Sure it was everyone for himself, but it was also everyone for everyone else. Natasha stretched from her nap, bunched muscles rippling like sunrise shimmering the sea. As we addicts linked hands to pray, I felt the weight of my gun deep in the lining of my longcoat, and I knew that God, whoever or whatever, good old God, was watching over me. In all His infinite mercy and wisdom, God was covering my ass.

49

CRACKERJACKS everywhere. I could spot them a block away, the loosey-goosey walk, the flexomatic necks, the paranoid pinball eyes, the me-Tarzan chest-beating able-to-leap-tall-buildings-in-a-single-bound Superman syndrome. Next to them, good old-fashioned heroin addicts seemed like nuns, calm and self-contained within their habits. I leaned against the phone stall on St. Mark's Place, Natasha motionless by my knee, watching the East Village flow: leather jackets, peacock-headed punks in fascist stompboots, soap-commercial scrubbed yuppies, snake-haired heavy metal kids, pale-as-death all-in-black Morticia Addams look-alikes with nose rings, homeless alcoholic street beggars with outrageous tales of woe and pleas for cash, crackerjacks and junkies, filthy deranged mutterers too far gone to beg, and the ever-present hordes of chattering Japanese fashion-victims wearing clunky clown shoes. Vendors everywhere, selling stolen goods: radios, bicycles, toasters, old clothes, records, books. Hell's Angels raced by on roaring Harleys. Drunken New Jersey Guidos with mousse-sculpted hairdos cruised slowly in made-in-the-U.S.A. muscle cars blaring rock, while black and Latino teenagers bopped by in rap-blasting Camrys, Saabs, and BMWs.

I read the *Post*. The death of Benito "Flaco" Jiminez on page fourteen. Flaco's transfer cried out for more than just a blurb. Three thousand plus vials of crack were found on the premises, yet there he was, buried on page fourteen, six lines and a cloudy picture, no suspects, no motive, banished to Palookaville by the legions of stories about billionaire builder Leonard Lump and his split from his East German swimmer wife, Svetlana (had she really taken steroids?), his "alleged" romance with "stunning starlet Sarah Syrup," reactions from friends, people in the street, gossip columnists, and Sarah Syrup's neighbors back home in Little Oblivion, Tennessee. For months the *Post* had written almost exclusively about the Lump carnival. Nelson Mandela had been liberated from prison. The iron curtain of communism had been torn down all across Europe. The seemingly invincible Mike Tyson had been defeated. The mayor of the nation's capital had been busted smoking crack. Panama invaded and Noriega jailed. Yet Leonard Lump, with his bushy brows and bulging bank account, had grabbed all the headlines, dwarfing world-shattering events as if they were no more important than TV listings. Fuck that billionaire pinhead. An alien spaceship could land in Times Square and no one would notice, if it happened to coincide with Leonard Lump's hemorrhoid operation.

Natasha growled. Some guy was staring at me funny. It was the cop from the meeting.

"Whattayasay?" he said.

"What's the word?" I answered.

"The name's Frank." He offered a hard hand.

"Ed." We shook.

"Yeah, I heard you sharin'. Fuckin' women are bitches, man. Wanna come for coffee? I'm meetin' a couple of sober fucks at Teresa's."

"Cool."

The cop and I walked in silence, smoking and spitting. It surprised me how comfortable I felt with him. I tied Natasha to a parking meter.

"Here, Ed." Frank foisted a slip of paper on me. "That's my phone number at the hotel, extension 407, if you ever need to shoot the shit." We entered the bright restaurant. "Ed, meet Billy B. and Rachel."

Rachel's hand was small and soft, strong and dry and electric.

Billy B. greeted me. "Life's got you sucking shit through a sock, huh Ed?"

"I'll take that as a compliment."

"Don't," said Rachel, laughing. And her voice was like a shot of cocaine in my groin.

"Bring me some of that crankcase oil you fuckin' call coffee." Frank winked at the waitress. "You guys?" It was unanimous. Crankcase oil all around.

"Frank," Billy B. said calmly. "Can't you be nice?"

"Pretty fuckin' impossible, Bill."

"I bet you really want people to like you," said Rachel. Her pouty-puffed kisser bloomed in a friendly smile.

"You're missin' the money, Rachel," Frank said, his ice-cold Aqua Velva-blue eyes staring her down. "I couldn't fuckin' give a shit what a bunch of delirious shitbirds flappin' their assholes in the breeze think. I don't need nobody."

"Mr. Macho," said Billy B. "If you don't learn humility, Frank, I'll lay odds you end up sucking shit through a sock."

"Y'know what, Bill?" Frank sneered. "Before I got suspended I used to eat disrespectful putzes like you for a snack. I once made a dealer-scum snort his stash of pink fuckin' flake coke till his fuckin' ears bled. Looked kinda like you."

"No shit?" Billy B. seemed amused.

"No fuckin' shit."

There was something about Frank I liked. It wasn't just his mastery of the language or how he hated dealers; there was a confidence, a seen-it-all take-no-shit quality that reminded me of some of the older guys in the navy.

"Why so quiet?" Rachel asked me.

I sipped crankcase oil.

"Just thinking," I said. And it was true. I was thinking. The old mind was winging away at warp speed. I was thinking that in some strange way Frank felt like an older brother. He was cop all right, but I liked him. And I was also thinking how amazingly good-looking Rachel was, about how lucky I was to be wearing my coat so no one could see the commotion in my pants; and to top off the top forty, I was thinking how could I get away from that tableful of lunatics to go smoke some yummy-yum crack.

"Excuse me," I said. "I have to call my sponsor."

I dialed Myron from the street.

"That you, Ed?" groaned my sponsor in a pained whisper.

"Myron, I miss my family."

"First things first. Did you make a meeting?"

"Yes, I did. Where were you?"

"I don't feel so hot. My period is coming on."

"Myron, you're a fifty-four-year-old man. Just because you wear women's clothes doesn't make you one."

He sighed. "Practice makes perfect."

"Jesus, you're fucking looney-tunes."

"Shut your mouth, beast. You think you can get on my good side with a bottle of expensive perfume and then abuse me? Let me tell you something, mister — I am woman, and I won't take shit from you or any man. How do you know what it's like for me? I have cramps, bad moods, bloating, pain —"

"I'm sorry."

"Sorry? You insensitive clod. You think 'sorry' stops my breasts from swelling?"

"I didn't mean to insult you. Please accept my apology. You're my sponsor. I need help."

"Oh, Ed." The anger had dropped from his voice. "You are a dear boy. Forgive me for yelling, but you don't know what it's like. My therapist says that when I get the operation I'll be okay; I'll have passed the change of life and can act my age."

"Myron, I feel like getting high."

"Turn it over."

"Myron?"

"What, Ed?"

"I feel like killing someone."

"That's a natural feeling. Go home and take a cold shower."

"I said kill, not fuck."

"Not this crazy bullshit again. Perhaps you ought to

get a male sponsor. The Program recommends the men sticking with the men. I'm not sure I understand these macho urges."

"But everything pisses me off. I just read the *Post* and I copped a resentment against Leonard Lump."

"You know what Farmer Rob said about resentment?"

"No, but I'm sure you'll tell me."

"He said: 'Resentment is like pissing all over yourself. Only you feel it.' Can you dig that?"

I was silent, digesting Farmer Rob's ripe produce.

"Ed, the war is over and you lost."

It was a nice idea, a really cute slogan, but Myron was wrong, dead wrong. The war had just begun.

Heading east into the Beirutal ruins of Alphabet City. Dealers clump-huddled on corners, hands shoved in pockets. Bums raking through garbage. Crackerjacks flicking Bics and hitting from stems, in doorways, down stairwells, in cars, mumbling "Beam me up, Scotty." Music bled from bars, from cruising cars. Sirens screamed: ambulances, fire trucks, and cop cars singing along in harmony. Mmm, that crack was gonna taste fine.

Natasha drew admiring whistles from many the Loisaida junkie and crackhead, yet none were dumb enough to pet her. They might be wacked out of their skulls, but their cruise-control instincts respected her knotted muscles and drooling alligator jaw.

On Avenue C, I passed a pair of Rastas smoking a cigar-sized spliff of fragrant herb. The smell drew me in, made me tremble with desire, as enticing as a Playboy Bunny in heat offering me a ride between her velvet thighs. But at what price? Just one hit? What would that do? Reefer hadn't ruined my life. I let Natasha squat and piddle, steam rising. The dreadheads' tomato-veined eyes stared at me dully. It was okay for them to get kite-high, but not me. I was a crackerjack. One hit of reefer and I'd be back sucking the Devil's Dick. I was working that Second Step, being restored to sanity by a power greater than myself, so I moved on, deeper into the barrio.

"Yo, homeboy!" cried a pencil-necked black guy walking toward me between avenues C and D. "Wha'sappenin'? What up? How many you need?"

"Funny you should ask," I said as the sweet jolt of excitement warmed my spine and tickled my guts. Just the idea of smoking got me high. I used to love this moment, that rich adrenaline high I felt when copping drugs on the street. You never knew if the shit was good or you were buying a crack vial full of soap or plaster. Anything was possible, the thrill of victory or the agony of defeat.

"Don't want any," I said.

"I axed you how many you need, not you want." My man saw the distinction.

"Thy will be done," I said, half under my breath.

"Whatchoo say? Don't be dissin' me, homes."

"I don't need anything."

"Whatchoo walkin' here, you don't be needin' nothin'?" His eyes were bugged out big-time. "I gots the nuclear jumbo."

"Fuck that jumbo, dumbo," I nastied back. "I don't smoke that shit."

"Then off my block, chump."

"This is still a free country."

Pencil Neck chuckled. "Land of the free, fag mafocka, home of the brave." He whipped a Rambo survival knife from under his fur-trimmed bomber jacket. "How mafockin' brave you be, homeslice?"

Natasha growled, the hair hackling her neck.

"I'll make shish kebab outta that piece-of-shit pit."

"She's an English bull terrier," I informed him, holding the straining rope.

"I don't care she the mafockin' Queen o' Inkland!"

"How many you need?" I asked, massaging the safety on the trigger of my deep-pocketed gun, turning the show over to my Higher Power. I'd go to any lengths to protect my sobriety.

"I'm the boss, whiteboy. Move the fock off." He waved his blade.

"How many you need?" I asked again, feeling a speedball mixture of calm and excitement in the face of his growing irritation.

The street was silent. The dark windows of abandoned buildings gaped blindly.

I backed a step off, but Natasha was rooted to the pavement. And then the barking.

"Shut that bitch up!"

"Freedom of speech," I said, above the frenzied yipping.

He stepped closer, knife flashing. "I ain't into games, punk. Time to get down."

I pulled the Glock, watched his face gawk. "Thy will be done," I said, and ended the mismatch with three quick slugs into his bomber jacket. There was something good and clean about the way the gun's force jerked my arm, something fine and artistic about the way he disco-danced down on the sidewalk, something sad and beau-tiful and ultimately spiritual about the way his eyes blinked rapidly, his stiffening fingers touched the holes in his leather, and he managed to say, "Beam me up, Scotty."

SITTING at the kitchen table, morning sun washing my face, three thousand-odd dollars in front of me, sharpening my new Rambo knife to Wilkinson razor quality, feeling peaceful, spiritual, no longer obsessed with sucking the Devil's Dick. The crack compulsion had been lifted, replaced by something far stronger. Both times I had killed, the desire to get high had been obliterated — snap! — soaked up like a spill at Rosie's diner. I felt cleansed, like I'd done the right thing. It didn't bother me one bit. Why, it was as comfortable as a long-lost pair of sneakers.

The apartment quiet. Gone the warm family feeling, the happy smiling faces. To be truthful, the last few years had been miserable, smiles definitely out of fashion. My wife's blond hair had grown lank from worry, her high-cheekboned Slavic face, with its blue eyes and kissable nose, gaunt and strained, wrinkles outstripping time, crowfooted and sad, a refugee from a Walker Evans photograph; and the boys, fighting all the time, bashing each other with Teenage Mutant karate chops, pulling lousy grades in school. Myron had told me that families pay the price of addiction. They disintegrate or go crazy. As long I kept clean, I'd never subject them to that torture again. Okay, so I'd lost the three people I loved most in the world, but goddammit, life was one big lost-and-found department. I'd find them again.

No television, no stereo, no radio: all sold for crack. I stared onto the Bowery. A few early windshield washers squeegeed morning cars. Another sunny day in Crack City.

The telephone bell cut through my blues like a chain saw through the Mormon Tabernacle Choir.

"Hello," I said into the chilled plastic receiver.

"Yo, Ed?" It was my running partner, Kenny, a photojournalist and 24/7 junkie-crackhead.

"Yeah, Ken."

"Crackadoodledoo!" he crowed, and the familiar greeting was like a hot rush of crack to my heart. "Doesn't sound like you, bro. You got a cold?"

"Got a cold cold heart," I said, trembling. And a warm warm gun.

"Can I come up? Need to talk."

"We're talking." Had to steer clear of people, places, and things that might bring up urges. Kenny was my best get-high buddy, as dangerous to my sobriety as Roman Polanski to a convention of Girl Scouts.

"Come on, brother mine, lemme in from the cold. Got some kicking dope and two jingling jumbos ripe 'n' ready for beaming."

"I'm straight, Kenny." Keep it steady, Eddie.

"You? Eddie T——? The original rebel without a pause? Come on, man, don't dis me, I'm freezing my black ass off. Been on a serious mission."

"You're a regular kamikaze. Can't let you up, blood. You're a walking-talking drug scene, and I got the disease."

"You got the AIDS?"

"No, the disease of addiction. I'm a fucking drug addict."

"Who the fuck isn't? Man, you can't escape the scene. We're living in Crack City. You might get off the shit, but the shit won't get off you."

"Kenny, I've got problems."

"I'll say you do — you're a foul-weather friend. Turning down a free bottle of rock and letting your brother get his eyes pecked out by the winterhawk. It's fifteen fucking degrees out —"

"Michelle left me."

"I know."

"You know?"

"I saw her over on the West Side."

"Going for the Greyhound back to her parents. With the boys."

"No, man, this was nighttime, no kids, and she was dressed all wild and shit, like a ho'."

"Kenny, man, Scotty's got you." I laughed at the ludicrous image. "Must have been someone else."

"Ed, how long we friends? Since B.C., kool. I know Michelle. It was her. I took pictures. And yo, she wasn't by the Port Authority. She was on the stroll, by the Convention Center. And now — now I'm gonna get high."

"Ken?"

He was gone.

I dialed Myron.

"Morning, Ed. I'm just off to work."

"Myron, a friend said he saw my wife on the street. I thought she was in Michigan with her folks."

"Does your friend do drugs?"

"Is Elvis dead?"

"There's your answer. He hallucinated it. Keep it simple, stupid. Easy does it. Don't project."

"Myron, later."

"Ed, let go and let God."

I dialed Michigan.

Ma Kawalski answered.

"Ma, it's Ed."

"Howdy," she said, distant as the Christmas-after-next.

"Put Michelle on."

"She's not here."

"She's got to be. Put her on."

"She's not here."

"I want to talk to her."

"She's not here, Ed. We heard you were, uh, ill."

"Where is she?"

"With friends in New York."

"What friends?"

"Give her time and space. She'll come back. How you feeling, son?"

"Meanwhile, where the fuck are my boys?"

Pa Kawalski's gruff old-soldier voice broke in. "Watch your language, boy."

I hung up. Or should I say, I hung the fuck up. I dressed quickly, packing my gun, my knife, putting Natasha on her rope. With friends? What friends? She didn't have friends. I went to the closet for my hat. Baseball gloves, bats, hockey sticks, skates. A bag of summer clothes. Bottles. Empty bottles. Empty vodka bottles. Five, ten. Vodka? I drank whiskey. Michelle barely drank a glass of wine a month. Vodka? A secret drinker? Dressed like a hooker? What the fuck was going on?

NINE A.M. Natasha and I trucked fast. Crack vials glinted in the bright sun. Glassine heroin papers whirled in the wind. Slices of newspaper skidded and sailed. Rats wiggled in and out of open garbage bags. Way uptown, in canyons of steel and stone, where deals were sealed with a wink and a drink, business was booming. Downtown, on Wall Street, college-educated cretins in thousand-dollar suits sweated out last night's cocaine-and-margarita festival, all prepped for action, sniffing lines to get the edge, to cut one another's well-shaved throats in order to climb the corporate monkey-ladder and make payments on their treasured BMWs, to buy grams of coke for a hundred bucks. In Loisaida, as in all the ghettos of Crack City, where fifteen-year-old dealers paid cash for their BMWs, drove them unlicensed, Uzis and nine-millimeters and double-pump shotguns under their coats, where dopefiends and crackheads kept their eyes peeled for their next rippable radio (to them, BMW translated as Break My Window), the coke and dope biz was well under way: bags of dope ten bucks, grams of blow as low as thirty, crack everywhere, at the universal price of five bucks a vial. It was a bullish market. Buyers

64

and sellers strolled the streets, picked sleep snot from puffy eyes, sipped coffees or brown-bagged beers, smoked cigarettes, discussed the merits of "What's good today?" Shoppers formed lines for their favorite brands, as orderly and polite as Russians line up for toilet paper. Addicts of every race, color, and creed equal under street law, the democracy of compulsion: you pay your money, you get your fix.

I couldn't get Kenny's strange message out of my head. Michelle dressed like a hooker? The mother of my children? First things first: find Kenny.

I burst through the unlocked green door of the abandoned building, blew by the nodding sentry, took the stairs two at a time, kicking garbage, sidestepping slush-puddles of puke. Opened the gallery entrance. Bars of sunlight streamed milkily through windows cataracted by dust. Junkies lay nodded out on ratty mattresses, dreaming about Bermuda and mother's milk. Cracker-jacks hit from stems, murmuring, "Beam me up, Scotty." The rough wooden floor littered with candy wrappers, crack vials, and heroin envelopes. The stench of dried blood, sweat, and decay filled my nose and throat.

"Yo, man! You can't bring no dog in here." This from a skyscraper brother in leather bomber jacket, gold chains, backward blue Mets cap, Oakley shades, and brand-new unlaced Air Jordan sneakers.

"You got a health code?"

"Shee-it, homeboy, dog ain't sanitary. I don't want nobody gettin' sick." He smiled wide. Sunlight flashed off a diamond-starred gold front tooth. "I'm the new manager here, just doin' my job."

Natasha sensed antagonism. The short hair on her

neck bristled straight up like a new toothbrush. She pulled at her rope.

"You tell her that," I said.

"Just this once, homeboy. Next time no dog. That'll be ten bucks cover."

I reeled Natasha in, peeled a bill, paid the man. Fucking Mets fans.

In the next room, an old junkie squatted in the corner over a frying pan, wiping his withered butt with the cover of a yellowing *Post*, a picture of Leonard Lump. Further into the gallery, past guys cooking dope in Budweiser quart bottlecaps, guys with belts tied round bruised puny needle-tracked arms, guys and gals pumping veins and jabbing with the weeper, I found Kenny, stem in mouth, beamer in hand, used syringe and burnt spoon by his side. He looked bad, even worse than I'd seen myself in the mirror before I went into detox. Lips cracked, covered with sores, hands blistered and burnt from handling hot stems. He was thin and brittle-looking, his copper skin tinged green, his brown eyes ghoulish, his shoulder-length dreadlocks sloppy and greasy, a camera slung round his neck.

"Crack is wack," I said.

"Yo, bro. Crackadoodledoo!" His eyes focused. "Scotty is dotty, liquor ain't quicker, whole lotta junkies born in Porto Ricker. Who's the girlfriend?" He limply touched my drooling darling.

"Time to bust out of here, Ken."

"No way, José. This my home sweet home away from home."

His eyes clouded over like glazed doughnuts.

"Show me those pictures you say are Michelle."

"Shit, Eddie T., maybe this crackerjack got it wrong. Could be that wasn't your lady."

"Either way, I want them. Gimme."

"At the lab. Didn't have the energy to do it myself."

Kenny was nodding, head wobbling. He flicked his Bic and sucked the Devil's Dick for a good fifteen seconds, lovingly stroking the blackened glass tube with orange flame, the coke crackling. He held the smoke down, eyes bugging, then loudly exhaled a cloud, like a steam engine at rest. He held his right thumb up. It was swollen.

"I got crack thumb, man," he said, getting on all fours and scoping the floor close up. "Score!" he cried happily, finding a white rock, putting it into the stem, and beaming it. "Yecchh." He spat. "Fucking plaster."

I plucked the hot stem from his fingers and threw the fucker hard across the room, where it shattered.

"Dust to dust," I said, and pulled him to his feet.

"I wanna stay," he whined.

"Can't always get what you want. You need fresh air."

From behind me came the measured tone of the big guy.

"Man wants to stay, man says. Free country and whatnot."

I turned, letting Kenny fall with a thump.

"Mind your own fucking business, Too Tall."

"Say, Dudley Doright, this is my business. The brother stay, he buy more rock, more dooge, another stem and beamer, more works. Dr. K's a steady customer. Translation, dumb-fuck: dough-ray-me. You read? This ain't no day care center."

He sure wasn't a pip-squeak. Six six, two fifty.

"Business must be bad, you care so much about one motherfucker."

"No, my European brother, business is beautiful. And so's your dog. Black. Beautiful black dog, ugly-ass whiteboy: bad match. Yo, I'll buy her from you." Natasha yanked at the rope. Too Tall whipped a wad of bills from his jacket. "How much? Two hundred? Three hundred? I'm livin' large. Fine female like that worth big money."

"Put the green away, lardbucket. You can't buy love."

He smiled, sunlight glinting off his special tooth and space-age shades, put the money back, and his paw came out for the second act with a little silver gun.

"How 'bout we simplify things?" he asked with a jewel-toothed grin.

"How 'bout we let the lady in question decide?"

I dropped the rope. Natasha torpedoed across the room, vaulted at Too Tall's gun hand, getting wrist, sharkteeth locking hard and fast. He yelped, dropped the piece, staggered into the wall, smacked his head. The shades flew off and he went down like a big sack of onions, Natasha landing catlike on her feet, clamped on, blood on her lips. Too Tall screamed. My girl whined with pleasure, grinning, grinding, shaking, blood now pouring, bones crunching. She shook her head side to side, up and down, flinging the gold-ringed hand, gritting her powerful jaws, growling, grating bone, muscle, and tendon, slicing veins, shaking. Too Tall grabbed her collar and tried to pull her off, hit her tough clubbing blows that might have been mosquito bites for all she noticed. Soon he tired, and as she shook and shook, blood gushing into a puddle, their mutual moans took on an almost sexual tone, a harmony of her pleasure and his pain.

"Let go and let God," I said to Natasha, grabbing her collar. Kenny was having a vomit in his corner.

I pulled hard. And that did it. Natasha came free. One problem: so did Too Tall's hand. Blood spurted from the jagged red stump. The big man shrieked, loud and long, high like a soprano. Natasha stood there panting, head cocked, staring at him curiously, the gold-ringed hand in her mouth like a souvenir, dripping blood onto the floor. Junkies and crackerjacks crowded around. Kenny wiped his mouth and started snapping pictures.

Too Tall moaned. His arm gushed. I sidestepped the thickening puddle, reached into his bomber jacket and relieved him of his cash.

"You won't need this where you're going," I said, soft and doctorlike. "There's no cover charge."

"Get an ambulance," he begged, shock coating his eyes, the red pool spreading.

"Holy shit," said Kenny, clicking away.

"You think you're ready to leave home now?" I asked.

The gallery customers cleared a path, and as we left, they descended on the big man, like pigeons on bread crumbs, stripping him of gold, crack, heroin, lighters, works, stems, sneakers, and jacket.

I looked back. One enterprising fellow, wearing Too Tall's Mets cap and sunglasses, was carefully tapping at his gold tooth with a Budweiser quart bottle. These days, everyone's a dentist.

Oᴜᴛ behind the abandoned building, in the trash-strewn broken-brick rubble where the wrecker's ball had obliterated tenement housing, where the Dracula developers would soon erect condominiums for overpaid pencil-pushers, under the bright winter sky, Natasha just wouldn't drop her prize, Too Tall's slowly dripping hand. Gold rings sparkled on the dark fingers. Kenny snapped pictures.

"That's it!" he exclaimed, as if shooting a fashion spread. "Look this way. More smile. Okay, pat her." He grunted approval as I knelt against cold brick and smoothed Natasha's soft-coated flanks. "This'll make a fantastic postcard."

"Cut the shit, Kenny," I said. "This isn't for publication." I pulled the cold hand. "Natasha, drop it." She didn't want to relinquish the fruits of her hard labor. "Let go and let God," I commanded, working the Third Step of Hard Drugs Anonymous. "Let go and let God, Natasha." She shook her head, the blood caked and frozen on her jaws.

"She likes pizza, Ken. Go grab her a slice."

I breathed deeply. The air tasted sweet after the stuffy

70

coffin stink of the gallery. I felt great. Alive. Weak in the knees, like an adolescent stumbling down whorehouse stairs.

"How about this?" he asked, pulling a stuffed animal from the wreckage of twisted pipe and crushed red brick, dusting red powder from a football-size plump lamb, threadbare, earless, "wool" rubbed thin from some kid's fondling. Child cries, "Mommy, Mommy, I left Larry Lamb." Then the huge metal ball crashes the building. Bricks erupt. Wood beams splinter. Dust and destruction. Like Dresden after the bombs. Wiped out: walls that had witnessed generations of immigrant life. Dreams, sorrows, fights, sex, painful births and painful deaths: hard lives. All gone. Now all that remained of a hundred years of history was a cute and cuddly stuffed animal.

"Natasha, kill this," commanded Kenny, tossing the toy.

She examined it, dropped the hand, poked and sniffed with her nose, then gently plucked the lamb up. Kenny pounced on the hand, pulled rings from fingers. "Cheap gold." He sighed. "Be lucky if I get thirty bucks."

We strolled over to Tompkins Park, stopping for coffee, cigarettes, a box of dog food, and a *Post*. Natasha kept squatting and peeing.

"She got a bladder problem?" asked Kenny.

"No, man, she's just leaving her business card."

We parked ourselves on a bench near Bushville. The homeless were already passing quart beers and warming their hands over garbage can blazes.

"Look at that shit." I pointed at the *Post*.

"Already read it. Motherfucking Leonard Lump."

71

Ken shook his head at the cover picture of the billionaire singing at the funeral of his fun-loving fellow richie-rich Malcolm Forbes, Lump's mouth open, his hair windswept.

"I heard he never sleeps," I said, basting my throat with coffee, ripping open the box of pooch pellets. "Probably a coke freak."

"Who needs sleep" — Kenny lit my Marlboro and his own Kool with his beamer — "when you're living in a dream world?"

"You didn't really see Michelle out hooking, did you?"

"It sure looked like her."

"Did you say anything?"

"Couldn't. Snapped a few shots, then she jumped into a telephone company truck."

We smoked, watched Natasha gobble her breakfast.

"You miss writing?" he asked.

"I did, until I got clean. Now I don't give a shit. I just want to find Michelle and the boys and get the hell out of Dodge."

"I gotta hand it to you," he said, laughing. "That was quite a scene back there." He wagged his head admiringly, gave three cigarettes to a snot-mustached egg-bearded ragamuffin who stood in front of us making smoking gestures.

"Kinda made me feel good," I said. "Motherfucker was asking for it."

"He sure got it. I'll bet he's eating Cheerios with Lucifer right now. Maybe someday you'll write about it."

"Maybe," I agreed, lighting another Marb. "For now, though, the sword is mightier than the pen."

"Used to be the other way around, bro. Fucking *New York Post.*"

There it was, the unsaid. We tried never to talk about it. How we'd been fired from the *Post* after getting bumped from real news to bullshit. How I ended up penning recipes for beef goulash. How Kenny was sent to photograph baby polar bears.

"Fucking *Post.*" I shook my head.

"You see where this Spanish brother got poked in the eye with a stem? Cat named Flaco?"

"Alas, poor Flaco, I knew him well, Kenny. Wholesaler."

"And you didn't turn me on to the connection?" He sounded hurt.

"Hey, bro, do I know all your sources?"

"You got a point. Too bad I didn't take the picture. Would've been perfect for my book."

"How's the book coming?" I asked.

"Oh, man, it's wild! I'm calling it *Crack City.* What else? This town is fucking infested. I've been on a month-long run, Ed. Buying drugs, doing drugs, hanging in crackhouses, shooting galleries. Getting blowjobs from crackwhores. Why do you think all crackwhores have potbellies? Malnutrition, man. And they all call Scotty 'The Master' or 'The Great Deceiver.' Man, you wouldn't believe how this city revolves around crack and heroin. Lawyers and execs sitting on their briefcases sucking that Devil's Dick right alongside pickpockets and pimps. Mothers selling their baby carriages for two vials. Grandmothers turning tricks. Sixteen-year-olds making two grand a day dealing. Kids with guns shooting each other for sneakers. It's the real deal, my brother. Gonna be a terrific book."

"Kenny, you look like shit."

"Yo, man!" He laughed, raking his dreadlocks. "I sacrifice vanity for art. This girleen I tore up last night had no complaints. She was sucking the Devil's Dick while mine was up her —"

"The shit's killing you, bro. Was killing me. Why not get straight?"

"Straight?" He shivered. "I haven't been straight since 1972. Ask me again when the book is done."

"Then you admit you have a problem?"

"Yeah. I ran out of money."

I peeled him two hundred plus from Too Tall's roll.

"Good looking-out!" He licked his lips and stashed the cash.

"How 'bout getting some help, Kenny. Recovery is cool."

"Yo, don't inflict your recovery on me, Eddie T."

"Come with me to a meeting. Hard Drugs Anonymous. You might dig it."

"Those communist Moonie motherfuckers? I need that evangelical horseshit like I need a crack stem in the eye. Thanks, but no thanks."

"In God's time, my brother."

"Yo, Ed, I had enough God shoved down my throat for a lifetime when I was a youngblood. Anyway, I'm too busy. There's a whole city full of drug action and wack violence I've got to get down on film. It's my duty, bro, for history."

KENNY and I parted, agreeing to hook up later so he could give me the pictures of Michelle. I dialed Myron at work.

"Mr. Pitlik's office. May I help you?"

"Hi, Myron. Ed here. How's my sponsor?"

"Oh, Ed, the cramps, the cramps. You can't imagine the cramps."

"I've been married for twelve years. I can imagine." I lit a smoke. "My wife's a hooker."

"But how are you?"

"How am I? I feel like killing her."

"First things first: did you make a meeting?"

"I'll go tonight. Myron, you know what? I really believe that Third Step is running my life. Like God is setting up situations and I just react to them."

"That's all any of us can do. Ed, I'm really proud of you. You're getting The Program. Yes, it's difficult, but sugarpie, it's worth it. The serenity you feel when you stop trying to run the show is so exciting. One of the biggest obstacles to recovery is what Big Jim called 'self-will run riot.' Don't try to do it your way. Trust the process. Each day clean and sober is a gift from God."

"I'm scared of what I'll do when I find Michelle."

"Don't be scared. As Farmer Rob said, 'Inhale faith, exhale fear.' Comprendo?"

"One more thing."

"Sure."

"When I'm at the meetings, I look around and think: These people are truly crazy. Here they've been clean and sober a long time, and they're still bugged out of their minds."

"Don't take anyone's inventory but your own. Focus on yourself. Don't compare; identify. You'd want them to have compassion for you, so have some for them. Do unto others as you would have them do unto you."

"Did Farmer Rob say that?"

"Don't be such a smartass. Everyone recovers at a different pace. Farmer Rob once said, 'The disease is democratic. It doesn't discriminate. It wants all of us dead. It's cunning, baffling, and powerful, an equal-opportunity illness.' First things first. Worry about Ed. And remember what Big Jim said: 'Some are sicker than others.'"

"Myron, I don't know what to do with myself."

"Sure you do, Ed. Just keep doing what you've been doing. You're doing great. You're one of the lucky ones — you've been spared decades of torment. Enjoy it. Go take a walk in the park. It's a gorgeous day."

Natasha and I strolled through Central Park. How different it was from my childhood, when the place was one big reefer-and-acid party, a great surging sea of hairy hippies preaching peace, love, and togetherness, passing joints and jugs of wine. Now it was full of homeless people with bags full of refundable cans digging through garbage, like everywhere else in Crack City, homeless folk, crackheads, joggers, and rats scavenging alongside squirrels.

I hated the disease. It had stolen my family. A disease I couldn't see or anticipate, like a black-clad ninja in the night, ever watchful, patient, ready to pounce and shove a shiv in my liver, upset the applecart of my Program.

Sweet Natasha, her little lamb friend clamped softly between blood-caked sharkjaws. Together we were wading through the festering contagious stink of Crack City.

In the Ramble, a wooded hilly section of the park where gays met to grapple back in the bushes, I sat on a bench and sparked a Marlboro. Natasha dropped her lamb and licked my hand. I petted her rocky hammerhead. I was powerless. The only thing I could do was make my meetings, call Myron, just keep doing what I was doing, fighting the good fight, a soldier in the war on drugs. For every vial of crack sold, there was a baby crying for food. For every bag of dope sniffed or shot, there was a family fragmented, a spirit suffocated. Motherfuckers getting rich off pain and death.

"Got a match, dude?" asked a pasty-faced white slimeball with crack-buggy eyes, bomber jacket open over white shirt.

"Sure," I said. "Just stay away from the dog."

He fished a Bic from his pocket. "That's cool. I found one." The butane flame jumped a good six inches, like any righteous beamer, and he sucked smoke from a Newport. "Don't leave home without it."

"Yuk yuk yuk," I said.

"Just making small talk." He pretended to be hurt. "My name's Oscar, dude, like the award."

"Charmed, I'm sure."

"What you here for?" he asked.

"Peace and quiet."

"Yo, dude, don't feed me that. You wanna relax, you stay at home." His insect eyes peered curiously and his voice went hard. "You want drugs or sex you come sit on a bench in the Ramble. What are you, a cop?"

"What if I told you I was just a normal red-blooded American crackhead looking to get high?"

"I'd say, leave the fuckin' dog, dude, and come with me into the woods."

I roped Natasha to the bench and followed him into the bushes and trees.

"Okay, Satansucker," he said. "How many you need?"

"Need?"

"Dude, Oscar ain't no dealer for his health. I got payments to make on my co-op." He tossed his cig away and rubbed his crotch. "Lookee, you blow me and I'll give you a break, ten for forty bills. That's a great deal — you save ten bucks."

"No such thing as a free lunch?"

"Yo, Mary, I got nine-year-old boys in the Bronx lining up to eat me for one fuckin' vial."

"No shit?"

"No shit, Sherlock."

I gripped the Glock in my coat pocket and smiled.

"On your knees, Mary," he ordered, unzipping his

pants and yanking a nickel-plated .22 from his belt with the other.

"Saturday night special on a Tuesday afternoon?"

"On your knees and blow."

"How 'bout I blow you away?"

He sneered, mouth twitching. "Trouble is my middle name."

"Guess what?" I grinned at the gun pointing at my heart, as I aimed my piece at his chest through my pocket, remembering what Myron had said about doing unto others. "Trouble is my first name."

I pressed the safety on the trigger and pumped six delicious slugs into his chest. He did the puppet dance and fell, crimson splattering his front like a Jackson Pollock painting, his trigger finger tightening and loosing one shot into the air.

"You win the award, Oscar. Best choreography." I chuckled. "Don't trouble Trouble or Trouble will trouble you."

"My dick is cold," he moaned from the ground, sunlight splashing his red-soaked shirtfront.

"There'll be a lot of lonely nine-year-olds in the Bronx tonight."

"Why, dude, why?" he groaned, chest making shlurping noises.

"Ours is not to reason why, ours is but to dude or die."

"Why me?" His perplexed bug-eyes grew soft.

"Why not you? Don't beat yourself up about it." And as he died, his left hand raised and shot me the bird. I didn't like that, not one bit. What a cheeky bastard. I dusted him, I deserved the last word. So I whipped my razor-sharp Rambo knife out and sliced the offending finger off at the base, stuffed it in his mouth. The blood rolled down the finger and painted his lips red, dribbled onto his chin.

"Suck on that, Mary," I said, and went on about the business of early sobriety.

STANDING there that evening on St. Mark's Place, looking at the pictures, I cried. Michelle in breast-bulging leather halter under a short jacket, wearing spandex tights — stomach bare, eyes crazed — laughing with the hookers, dealers, and pimps on Eleventh Avenue, the slimy pimpled underbelly of Crack City, U.S.A.

"Why?" I wailed, attracting barely a glance from the crowds whizzing to and fro like sperm under a microscope.

"Ed, she's a chucklehead," said Kenny, rubbing his runny nose. "You're better off without her."

"What about my kids?"

"Never fear, Kenny's here. Bet, I'm a crackerjack detective. I'll find those little terrorists. Now you be a good little Moonie and run along to your cult meeting. I'll call. Just don't let those sober motherfuckers brainwash you."

"Maybe my brain is dirty; maybe it needs washing."

"Ed, chill out with that shit. Next you'll be selling roses at the entrance to the Lincoln Tunnel. I'll call you."

I headed to the meeting with Natasha, Larry Lamb still stuck in her jaws, her spindly legs carrying her cannonball bulk gracefully. My own wife, a hooker. Sure

I'd been no day at the beach — but I hadn't been a bad person. I'd been sick, diseased by drugs. How could she spread her legs for total strangers, for any alien wang with cold cash?

"Why me?" I wept within the warm smoky confines of HDA, as Program people kissed and hugged and shared slogans.

"Why the fuck not you?" asked Frank the cop, puffing a Camel. "Consider yourself lucky. You could be lyin' flat on your back in the fuckin' morgue." He filled a cup of coffee for me from the urn and then one for himself. "Go ahead and cry. It's fuckin' good for you."

"I feel like an asshole," I said, embarrassed by the waterworks, drying my cheeks, sipping coffee.

"Hey, pal, cryin' don't make you any less a man." The cop patted my back with a callused mitt. "I fuckin' done it plenty myself. Gettin' clean is no fuckin' bed of roses. My ex-wife fucked with me bigtime."

"Yeah? Did you feel like someone gave you a molten-lava douche?"

"Somethin' like that, yeah." He shuddered. I really did feel like shit, stomach all knotted and legs weak. A hundred-and-eighty-degree difference from the glorious soaring sensation I'd had earlier in the day after dispatching that slime Oscar.

"Ed, we got to fuckin' learn to love ourselves before we can love anyone fuckin' else. Maybe it's a blessin' she's gone. Look at it as the glass is half fuckin' full instead of half fuckin' empty."

My chest was heaving. The public fountain was gearing on up for another exhibition.

"I gotta split," I said.

"Stay. Big fuckin' Jim used to say, 'We can do what I cannot.' Don't fuckin' cut out, man. These assholes are your family. People cry here all the time. It's a regular Niagara fuckin' Falls."

"I hate being a goddamn baby," I said, backtracking to memories of my old man, how he couldn't stand me crying.

"You're not a fuckin' baby." He gently touched my shoulder. "You're like me, a sensitive fuckin' guy."

"Ed!" It was Myron, looking stylish in a lemon-yellow jumpsuit. "What's wrong, sugarpie?"

"His old lady's a dirtbag hooker," Frank told him. "She's out there suckin' off tourists and truckdrivers."

"It's part of God's plan," soothed Myron, leading me to a seat.

"You don't understand," I burbled.

He pulled me to his Obsession-fragrant cheek, laid my head against his pubescent breast. "Cry, baby, cry. Get it out. Your tears are but the icicles melting from your heart."

Myron stroked my hair. Natasha licked my hand. The speaker's words whistled by. Faces were blurred. All I could see was Michelle's hair teased into ringlets, her lovely body decked out in spandex booty pants and hooker armor, for sale on the streets of Crack City.

"Don't beat yourself up about it, Ed," whispered Myron. "Take the toilet paper out of your ears and listen."

". . . and until I took the Fourth Step, until I honestly focused on myself," said the speaker up front, a white woman in her forties wearing a McDonald's uniform, "I was the most miserable recovering crack addict on the planet. I worked on Wall Street. Made tons of money.

Had credit cards. Two BMWs. Three lovers. And no
friends. I dreamed every night that I was sucking the
Devil's Dick, that Scotty was calling for me. I had to
take a complete and brave moral inventory of my life to
find out who I really was. I had to come to terms with
my childhood, with feelings I had growing up in a dysfunctional family. I had to peel the smelly layers of the
onion to discover the lovely flower within. If you've ever
worked with onions, you know how many tears are in-
volved. I went through box after box of Kleenex. When
I took the Step, I was clean but had no serenity. I was
on a dry high. Now I'm grateful to slap pickles on your
Big Mac. I don't need money to live a good life. I only
need moral purpose, and I get that here in HDA. Today
I don't get high, and I help another sick and suffering
addict. I live life on life's terms. Before, I was a rich shit
isolated in a penthouse. Now I'm a flower, a beautiful
lotus. Oh yes, the flower emerged from the shit. The shit
fertilized the flower, but you all nurtured and watered
the flower, gave it the sunshine and care, not to mention
the coffee, it needed to blossom and grow. You all are
winners. I love you and thank you for my recovery."

I sobbed through the anniversaries, the ninety days,
the standing ovation Loo! Loo! Loo! received for making
his ninety.

"My name is Frank, and I'm a fuckin' drug addict and
alcoholic."

"Hi, Frank."

"Yeah, I'm fuckin' clean and sober and I feel fuckin'
great. I watched the news at six and guess what? Fuckin'
crack dealers are gettin' wacked right and fuckin' left.
And in fuckin' Manhattan! The fuckin' media don't give

a pistachio-nut shit when it goes down in fuckin' Brooklyn, the Bronx, or Queens; and Staten Island might as well be Bora fuckin' Bora for all anyone cares. I ain't stuffin' my feelin's on this one, baby. I feel fuckin' great. I say let those fuckheads cancel each other out, one slime at a time."

The cop was grinning, happy. I'd made his day. I felt a little better. I had a new friend.

"My name is Myron," my sponsor announced, "and I'm a grateful recovering alcoholic."

"Hi, Myron!"

"Thanks for your qualification, Betty. You've been a great power of example to me, a good friend, and we wear the same dress size. When you gave me the Halston to wear at my son's wedding, I felt so pretty, so special. It was a great day for me. You look really well and you have a powerful message. Thanks, honey."

"Thank you, Myron. My first sponsor used to call HDA 'Drugnet,' and she was fond of saying, 'Just the feelings, ma'am.' I'd like to hear from that young man next to you. He seems to be in a ton of pain."

"My name is Ed, and I'm a stupid stinking drug addict and alcoholic."

"Hi, Ed!"

"Pain? How's this? My life sucks. My wife's a prostitute and I don't know where the fuck my kids are. Maybe I was immoral before, putting drugs before my family, but why am I being punished for it now? It's like a fishhook in my heart. I feel like Frank over there. Those fucking crack dealers deserve what they're getting. Line them all up and shoot. I hate those scumsuckers. I blame them for what's happening to me."

"Ed." Betty tried to placate me. "Don't beat yourself up about it. Your body is still going through changes from getting off drugs. It does get better. Hang in there. As Big Jim said, 'God doesn't put more on our plate than we can handle.' Give time time."

"My name is Rachel, and I'm a drug addict and alcoholic and a sleazy slimy sex addict."

"Hi, Rachel!"

"Thanks for your qualification, Betty: I really needed to hear it; and thanks for calling on me. I'm going through a really hard time. I almost went to bed with a complete stranger tonight. I met him on the street after work. Something about danger really turns me on. I was up at his house and suddenly I knew I had to tip out of there and make the meeting. So I ran over here and I'm really happy I did. Maybe I ought to do a Fourth Step on my recent breakup, find out why I'm so compulsive. Why I want to eat and screw so much. I know that these days, with AIDS out there, sportfucking is flirting with death. Maybe it's anxiety over work. I'm up for a role on a soap opera. I'd really like to quit my day job, but it pays the bills. Most of you know I'm a dominatrix, whipping guys and all sorts of stuff, but no sex, and I guess you wouldn't call it a really serene position, but I don't think it's immoral. I look at myself as a therapist. I like what you said about living life on life's terms. I'm just going to pray that I land the soap. And I'm going to try to be patient, wait for the next right relationship. Not just the next horny dude. The way I got propositioned after the meeting last night, I almost wonder if HDA doesn't stand for Hard Dicks Anonymous."

Beautiful? She had the kind of looks wars get started

over. In the years before I hit The Program, I thought the only people in HDA were scabby old junkies in raincoats. Looking at Rachel could make a hundred-and-one-year-old homosexual squirt his Fruit of the Looms. Despite my duty to get my sons back, to straighten my wife's hair and strip her of spandex and leather, despite twelve solid years of monogamy, I was developing quite a crush on that sleazy slimy sex addict across the room.

IF all the years of drugging and drinking hadn't nailed me into a coffin, all the cigarettes and coffee of sobriety sure would.

Frank drove. Natasha slept in the back, nuzzling Larry Lamb. The sober cop and I had hooked up after the meeting to drink coffee, to toast the death of crack dealers, and to look for my wife. He'd bought ten cups to go from a deli, and we were motoring around in his Firebird, slicing up and around the whore-clotted heart of Crack City, keeping our eyes peeled for Michelle.

"She's fuckin' great-lookin'," he stated.

"No kidding. I hope she gets that soap opera part."

"Not Rachel, numb-nuts." He jabbed at the picture of Michelle between us on the front seat. "Your wife."

"Oh yeah, her too." I had to sigh. "I can't believe she's a hooker."

"The husband is always the last to fuckin' know."

"How could she do it?" I pounded the dash.

"Easy fuckin' does it, Ed. Don't take it out on the car. No sense gettin' bent all out of shape. The Program is kinda simpleminded and shit, but those fuckin' slogans are a real help. Don't beat the shit out of yourself with a fuckin' lead pipe. Give time a little fuckin' time. Let fuckin' go and let fuckin' God."

Frank navigated the muscle car through traffic like an ambulance driver transporting a heart-attack victim, huffing Camels and cussing cabbies, drowning his tonsils with coffee as we zipped through the panoramic cityscape of X-rated movies, peepshows, legit theaters, hookers, pimps, dealers, and tourists holding on to their wallets. Michelle a secret drinker and a hooker? Okay, she hadn't been a saint when we met; not even a virgin. She'd been dancing topless in the Lolita Lounge to pay for ballet lessons and Blimpie sandwiches. Not exactly Mother Teresa, but a flatbacker?

"I was a pisspoor husband," I confessed. "Spent all our savings on drugs and neglected the kids. Lost my reporter job and wound up mopping floors in a peepshow."

"Michelle must have fuckin' loved that shit." He ripped open another container of coffee and gulped.

"She wouldn't even let me wear my sneakers into the apartment. Said they had junkie jizz all over 'em. Couldn't touch her, either. Thought I was getting boffed at work."

"Were you?"

"They were beautiful, Frank. All races, shapes, sizes. And after watching scumbags pulling their puds on the other side of the glass booth all day and night these babes were ready to party. I used to cop bottles of rock for them and we'd be beaming up all night long. Oh man, what a temptation. I was like a diabetic kid in a candy store. I didn't lay a finger on any of them. I was true blue with blue balls. You know what it's like living with a fine woman and not getting any? Like sucking shit through a sock."

"Hey, pal, I ID with you down the fuckin' line. I got divorced last year. Drove my ex batshit. Now she's shacked up with a fuckin' dentist. All because she stopped trustin' me. We were fuckin' high school sweethearts. She swore she'd love me for fuckin' ever. Then bing bang boom, after eighteen fuckin' years, the whole deal went sour and she takes me for half."

"What went down?"

"You know the routine, Ed. First she nags you about the hours. Then she wants a fuckin' kid. Then it's the fuckin' drugs. Then she can't live on a cop's salary. Then she's smellin' my johnson for extracurricular poontang. Then the headaches, the excuses, the 'I don't love you anymore that way' crap. And finally the bitch wants out. Nag nag nag. Drove me to a ten-bag-of-dope-a-day habit. She served me divorce papers when I'm in fuckin' rehab. Now the fuckin' twat lives in Massapequa fuckin' Park and her fuckin' dentist boyfriend drills cavities to keep her in fuckin' fur. And me, I'm on fuckin' suspension, collectin' disability — which she still gets half of — and I gotta live in a shithole. All I do now is read the fuckin' *Post*, which I can barely fuckin' afford, and go to fuckin' meetin's and drink fuckin' coffee. I tell you, after cryin' my fuckin' eyes out over that sticky-assed cunt, I sure ain't in a hurry for a fresh headache. All they fuckin' want is some shithead to trust."

"Stop the car."

"There she is," he sang, "Miss Afuckin'merica."

We were on Eleventh Avenue, south of the Convention Center. Michelle looked wacked out of her blondringleted skull, oblivious to the bitter wind blowing in off the Hudson. She stood there smoking a joint with a silver-wigged black girl in a fake fur jacket and white thigh-high boots.

"Stay put, Ed. I'll handle this."

Frank hopped out and approached.

"Hey, honey," I heard my wife say. "You want a date?"

"You, Tina Turner," Frank barked at the sister. "Take a fuckin' hike."

"This a free country!" she shrilled.

Frank pulled his jacket open and touched the butt of his holstered gun.

She shrugged, lowered her wig into the wind, and skipped off on bird legs to stand with a gaggle of working girls.

"Police officer," Frank said. "Get in the car, Michelle."

"How do you know my name?"

"I'm fuckin' psychic."

"You can't bust me, man. You don't have a thing on me."

"Look, lady, you barely have a thing on yourself. Come in the fuckin' car and get warm. Someone wants to talk with you."

She looked over.

"I'm not talking to him." Mouth grim.

"Wanna bet, bimbo?" He gripped her elbow and steered her over.

"Hello," I said, getting out, feeling shy. Frank went and sat on the hood, smoking.

"What do you want?" she asked, eyes slitted.

"What happened to your hair?"

"You tracked me down to ask about my hair?"

"It's different."

"It's a wig. The *Fatal Attraction* look." She laughed. Her pupils were pinpricked: heroin.

"You look like the Bride of Frankenstein."

"And you look like shit. What do you want?"

"Where are my sons?"

"You'll never know."

"Look, baby, I'm clean and sober. Please come home."

"I'm not a baby and that's not my home. I'm independent now. So, to quote yourself, get out of my face."

"When did you start getting high?" I asked, amazed at her new attitude.

"What does it matter? Look, Ed, we had some good years, but that's ancient history. I've got a new life. A career."

"Michelle, cut the shit. Come home and we'll work it out."

"I don't want to work it out. I went to one of those meetings for the families of addicts — what's it called, Junk-Anon? Christ, those people are miserable. But I did get something out of it. They told me that I didn't cause the shit, I couldn't change it, and I sure as hell can't control it. They told me that you kept me hostage, that you were a terrorist. They suggested I clear out."

"I'm begging you. Things will be different. I'm making money now. Meaningful work. I paid the rent and phone. I'm clean. Give me a fucking chance. I'm begging."

"Don't beg; it's disgusting. You had every chance and then some. Find another victim."

"One week, Michelle. I was in the hospital one fucking week. Why couldn't you wait for me?"

"You made the choice, Ed, years ago, and you picked drugs."

"You're willing to flush twelve good years down the toilet?"

"You're the one who flushed it all away. I tried. Lord knows I tried. Anyway, don't flatter yourself; they weren't so good. The marriage is kaput. I don't trust you."

"C'mon, Michelle." I was trembling. "Let's go home and forget this insanity."

"You go home. I'm happy right here."

"Where are Mutt and Jeff?"

"You mean Donatello and Jeff."

"Who?"

"Matthew doesn't like being called Mutt. He thinks he's a Teenage Mutant Ninja Turtle called Donatello."

"That's great. My son the turtle. Where're Jeff and the turtle?"

"Why should I tell you? So you can take them prisoner?"

"Because they're my sons. I'll find them, Michelle."

"Tiffany."

"Tiffany?"

"That's my new name."

"What's Jeff's new name?"

"Jeff is Jeff."

"I'll get them back."

"Over my dead body."

"That can be arranged."

"You made a damn good start of it back at Houston Street."

"Meaning?"

"You don't remember? You dumb junkie, that's why I left. You smacked me."

"I guess I was in a blackout," I said, surprised.

Her eyes were cold as reindeer nuts, and she mimicked me: " 'I guess I was in a blackout.' "

"Come home, babe. It'll never happen again."

"It'll never happen again because I'm never going back." Her chest was bumpy with chilled gooseflesh, her face splotched scarlet with anger.

"I love you."

She moved off, tottering on high heels.

"Michelle!" I called.

She reached her bottle-passing co-workers, turned, and smiled.

My heart did a teenage flutter.

"Fuck off," she said, raising the bottle to her lips and chugging. "Fuck off and die."

FRANK's room in the Duke o' Windsor Hotel was the size of an overweight basketball player's coffin, with chicken-wire ceilings. And it smelled. Of mold, mildew, old smoke, hot-plate cooking, industrial-strength foot rot, and ten thousand pukabilly drunks. Through the dim thin stained walls I could hear the moans of the sleep-tortured, the cackling of the crack-crazed, the wrenching phlegmish coughs of two-pack-of-Pall-Mall-a-day emphysemics sputtering away like a fleet of decrepit tractors starting up on a subzero Alaskan morning. Starting, failing, starting again. Concentrated sorrow compounded by anxiety, bad health, and mental illness. A whistle-stop on the road to death.

"A real fuckin' palace, huh?"

"It's not so bad," I lied.

"Yes it is."

"How long you been here?"

"Since the fuckin' divorce."

"Frank," I said, sitting on the rickety chair, Natasha panting slit-eyed at my feet, "if I lived here I'd shoot dope."

"I consider that fuckin' option every goddamn day."

The walls were plastered with newspaper photos and headlines from the past year. Bloody scenes of Crack City. Everyday life. Guns and drugs, robbery and riot and rape, drive-by killings. The usual. Above the headboard hung the freshest clipping, not yet warped by mildew or urine-colored by time: a shot of Flaco, his stem-stuck eye caked with blood, his ponytail still *GQ* perfect.

I complimented his interior-decorating taste: "Cheerful."

"You like them?"

"Yeah, man," I said, wanting to tell him all about it — the sweet electric jolt when the stem pierced Flaco's eye and cut the wires in his brain and the red lifejuice spewed — tell him how happy I was that he appreciated my artistry.

Frank grunted and hit the On button of a cheap black-and-white Zenith, fiddled with the hanger that served as antenna. The picture went from snow to blank to psychedelic. He batted the set with a meaty fist and the screen fizzed into focus.

"Piece of shit," he proclaimed.

The channel 7 newscaster had mismatched eyes. "Death came in a hail of bullets to Bronx resident Oscar LeBron in Central Park this afternoon. Forty-eight vials of crack and a weapon were found on the paroled child-molester's mutilated body, leading police to speculate —"

"How about that?" I asked, wishing I could share my secrets, hoping the glow I was feeling wasn't showing.

"Fuckin' A right!"

Frank opened the suitcase at the foot of the bed, shook a few dead cockroaches and mothballs from a cop's dress uniform, put on the blue cap and sat back against the gallery of rubouts, snorting smoke out his bushy nostrils.

"Baby-raper got what he deserved," he said. "I'm only sorry it wasn't me shot the scumbag." I had a vision of Frank and me tag-teaming up to wack crack dealers.

"You miss being a cop?" I asked, like a job interviewer.

"I was fuckin' born for it. My old man was a cop and so was his old man. I bleed NYPD blue. And I was a good fuckin' cop. Sent a lotta guys away for a lotta time. And I never got caught takin' a fuckin' payoff or rippin' off drugs."

"That's life," I said, my desire to confess shriveling up like gonads immersed in icewater. "You're only a fuckup if you get caught."

"One minute I'm a hero" — Frank sighed — "the next I've got a terminal fuckin' disease and I'm sittin' around HDA babblin' my ass off with a bunch of brain-dead crackheads."

"Learning to be humble," I reminded him.

"To fuckin' humility." We touched cardboard coffee cups. "So, Ed, your wife dissed the piss out of you, huh?"

"Fuck her." I hauled savagely on a Marlboro.

"She's a hot tomato."

"A rotten tomato."

"Hey, Ed, you're blushin'."

"I think it's called high blood pressure."

"Chill out, man. You know what Farmer fuckin' Rob said?"

"You can't get milk from a pig?"

"No, numb-nuts. He said, 'Take the action, let go of the result.' You said your piece. Now go about your fuckin' life. If the bitch won't play ball, find one who will. Maybe it just fuckin' wasn't meant to be."

He looked over at his bedside table and his eyes grazed on a cheaply framed photo of a big-haired Italian-style brunette.

"Your ex?"

"You got it, pal. My Excedrin PMS headache."

"Why keep her picture, Frank? Why not listen to your own advice and let go and let God?"

"In the words of the immoral Billy B., I like to suck shit through a sock." Frank pulled his hat off and stared at it. "I guess I'm full of self-fuckin'-hate. The bitch is fatal news for me — I know — just like fuckin' heroin and whiskey, but I still love her, still focus on the good times."

"What do you do for sex? Hookers?"

"Nah. Too expensive. Anyway, The Program says no relationships the first year clean. Nope, I went back to my first fuckin' love." He held his nicotine-stained right hand up for inspection. "Ed, meet Rosy Palm, the only bitch I ever had who never cheated on me."

"Uh, Frank, you'll forgive me if I don't shake."

No way could I face the apartment, that junkyard of memories. My wife a whore? Fuck her. Sleep? I'd drunk about fifteen cups of coffee. I had nothing but energy, energy and hate. A smorgasbord of evil thoughts jockeyed for position in my brain. Fuck her.

I ambled down the Bowery below Houston, Natasha stalking by my side, sleepy, her little lamb stuck in her chops.

We passed the hardiest of outdoorsmen, scabby faced bums too far gone for hotels or shelters, warmed only by bellies full of T-bird or Mad Dog wine, balled up newspapers sticking from layers of filthy rags, plastic bags wrapped around their feet. Homelessness: the last frontier. Meanwhile, somewhere high above Crack City, in an opulent penthouse with machine-scrubbed air and gilded toilets, refrigerators bulging with candied pheasants and chilled champagne, Leonard Lump and Sarah Syrup humped away like a pair of lubricated kangaroos on a trampoline, oblivious to the poverty and hunger and misery in the world below.

Filthy rotten city. Decaying metropolis riddled with death and disease. Garbage coating the streets. Broken

99

glass sparkling the black cracked asphalt. New York was cracked. America was cracked. The goddamn Liberty Bell was cracked.

Little Italy. Late-night dealers hung in doorways, fish-eyed, waiting like schools of snapjawed trout on the surface of a stream for their next fat bug-victim.

I dialed Myron at home.

"Where are you, Ed?"

"Somewhere between hell and Hawaii."

"How do you feel?"

"Dead inside. I saw Michelle. She's a prostitute."

"That's not your fault."

"But it is, Myron. She told me I hit her. Like my own damn father beat on my mother, I hit her. I drove her to drink. I drove her to drugs. I drove her to suck off strangers. The shoe fits."

"Ed, it's okay to make mistakes. Anyway, if you ask me, she chose it. This is an issue I'm familiar with. I spent the worst years of my life turning tricks."

"Speaking of neat tricks, how're the cramps?"

"Like your domestic situation, painful. But they will get better. Ed, Big Jim Williams was fond of saying, 'Halt. H-A-L-T. Never get too Hungry Angry Lonely or Tired.' Are you hungry?"

"I couldn't eat if Julia Child was cooking."

"Eat. Don't tempt the disease. Big Jim always carried candy bars."

"Is that how he got to be Big Jim?"

"Is something making you angry?"

"Was St. Francis of Assisi a pigeon-lover?"

"Don't be snide. I'm trying to help. You know, in the early days of The Program they called newcomers 'pigeons.' When a pigeon is hurt, the other pigeons care for it, feed it, lick its wounds till it can fly again. You're that wounded pigeon."

"A pigeon with a stick of dynamite up its ass. Myron, my life is falling apart, the whole fucking U.S.A. is a red cunt-hair away from self-destructing, and you hit me with the dumbest horseshit I've ever heard."

"Pray for relief from your rage. Let go and let God. Turn it over. You lost your best friends, booze and drugs. You lost your wife. Mourn them, and fill the void with spirituality. God can do for us what we cannot do for ourselves."

"These vapid clichés are beginning to wear thin."

"Don't beat yourself up about it. Talking the talk is one thing, but you have to walk the walk. Are you lonely tonight?"

"No, Myron. My wife's a hooker, my sons are missing in action, and I hang out with lunatics in HDA. I couldn't be happier."

"Where's your dog?"

"She's here."

"Sleep with her."

"That's a little kinky for me."

"Don't be such a smartass. These things work, they truly work. Are you tired?"

"I'm riding the caffeine Concorde. I couldn't sleep if you hit me over the head with a baseball bat."

"Ed, remember K-I-S-S. Keep it simple, stupid. Get some food, go home, play with your dog, and pray. 'Acceptance is the key.' That's what Big Jim said. Accept things as they are. Remember, God doesn't put anything on our plate that we can't handle."

*   *   *

The bells on the door of the little bodega tinkled like Santa's sleigh as I entered. I'd been there many a time. The Dominican behind the counter wore a slick silk shirt, gold chains buried in a carpet of black chest hair. He was watching "Lifestyles of the Rich and Famous." Robin Leach's annoying voice blasted out a laundry list of Germany's splendors. The proprietor recognized me and smiled behind his waxed mustache.

"Oye, hombre, wha' you need?" he asked loudly.

"Gimme a bundle." I pulled five twenties off my roll. Why not sniff some heroin? I had to accept the fact that I was a junkie, a stone-cold dead-souled junkie. The fucking Program wasn't working. If anything, it was making matters worse. All I was getting was heartache and heartburn and slogans. A little dope would smooth out the wrinkles. Life really did suck shit through a sock.

I passed him the money and he palmed me the dope, ten little opaque bags rubberbanded together, stamped with the brand name "McDonald's." Robin Leach swished vino around his mouth and praised "the fine Rhine wine of the nation that gave the world Marlene Dietrich and Wernher von Braun."

Then chaos. A large red Doberman rose barking against its chain behind the counter. Natasha dropped Larry Lamb, whined like a baby, pulled the rope from my hands and sprang over the counter, claws scrabbling wood. The Doberman slashed at her head with slobbered fangs. Tooth scraped bone, but Natasha went for the long neck, tore into it, clamped like a sprung beartrap onto the sweet section of the throat, shaking furiously. The

Dobie hit the floor, slashing still, making tortured noises as Robin Leach droned on.

"Tell her stop!"

"She's in love," I said, half watching the dogfight, half watching Robin sipping a sweaty stein of foamy beer in a leafy-treed Munich beer garden.

He kicked Natasha. Loud thump. He cracked her coconut skull with a sap. She paid no heed. The Doberman's jugular pumped blood like an open faucet. Natasha was locked on. I picked a jar of peanut butter off the nearest rack and threw. It glanced off the guy's head, smashed an autographed photo of Iris Chacon, coating the bikinied bombshell with brown glop and shards of glass. He reached under the counter, came up with a .38, pointed it woozily. I was over the counter, Rambo knife in hand, knocking Slim Jims and beef jerkies all over, driving the blade with force into his love zone, hearing the gasp, smelling garlic on his breath as I twisted.

"Mommy," he moaned, falling to the floor, blood spreading, staining his silk shirt, clotting his chest hair. I stepped on his wrist and kicked his gun away.

"Mommy!" he moaned again, hands groping his crucifix.

"Let go and let God, Natasha," I said, and she whimpered with the bloodlust, yanked the Doberman's neck.

I rifled the cigar box under the counter and came up with a few thousand in cash, took the guy's blackjack, yanked my knife from his heart, wiped it on his shirt, and pocketed some beef jerkies. Natasha still wouldn't loosen her grip, though the Doberman was past struggling, lying there, accepting death, feebly trying to lick its wheezing Mommy-moaning master. I grabbed Natasha's lamb, shook it at her. The glazed-crazed look faded from her eyes, and she let go. Spattered with blood, breathing hard, red hair on her tongue, a length of vein hanging from her teeth like used dental floss, she waded through a thin red pool to take her little friend between wet lips.

Leaving the store, I snagged a bag of Doritos. It was bad for my sobriety if I got too hungry. The door tinkled shut behind us. As I stood in the cold munching corn chips, Robin Leach's vulgar voice filled the stillness, bequeathing "Champagne wishes and caviar dreams."

I SAT drinking a Coke in the window seat at the Grass-roots Tavern on St. Mark's, watching late-night strollers and street scum slither by. Natasha lapped water from a beer mug. I wiped her blood-caked yap with bar napkins. People hoisted frosty brews, slammed mixed drinks, yelled, laughed, their red faces bloated and mapped with exploded capillaries. They looked stupid as shit. I didn't envy them one bit. I was off all the poisons, happy to be sober.

"How do you feel?"

I looked into a pair of deep black peepers. Rachel.

"Hello," I said. "I was drinking a Coke, no liquor."

"I saw you in the window. Can I sit?"

"By all means. Want a soda? Some beef jerky?"

"Thanks, no. Ed, I don't mean to preach, but if you don't want a haircut, you should stay out of barbershops."

"Maybe I'll grow one of those Hollywood ponytails."

"Please don't. How do you like being clean and sober?"

"It's just peachy, thank you."

"You really seem miserable at the meetings."

"My sponsor told me that was the local dump for pain."

"Ride that chair, cowboy."

"To tell you the truth, Rachel, things suck." I lit a cigarette from the one I'd been smoking. "At least I've got my health."

"I look into your eyes and I see a bottomless volcano of despair. It does get better."

"I know. Give time time. Easy does it. Don't pick up that first drug or drink. Keep coming back. Use the telephone. Trust the process. Turn it over. One day at a time. Don't stuff the feelings. Walk the walk. Let go and let God. Keep it simple, stupid. Arrest the disease. H-A-L-T. Acceptance is the key. Don't scratch your ass without calling your sponsor."

"You're learning fast." She laughed. "Honest, Open, Willing. That's H-O-W. That's how The Program works. You know, there are no coincidences in HDA. God put you in this window and made me walk down the street tonight. I believe that."

"You believe what?"

"God meant us to meet."

I felt a distant sub-zipper urging.

"You think so?"

"I know so. Ed, you need a hug."

She stood with open arms. Black leather jacket over white T-shirt vacuumed me to her springy breast. Her curly hair tickled.

"Mmm," she mmmed. "That's nice. Hugs not drugs."

"Yes." I sighed. "But . . ."

"But what?"

"Can I be honest with you?"

"This is a program of rigorous honesty."

"You're incredibly attractive, and for a long time, a very long time, my wife and I haven't . . . for a long time, and, well, it's been a long time, and . . ."

"Easy does it, Ed. I know exactly what you mean." She smiled. "You need a nude hug."

We forgot all about safe sex. "Daddy, Daddy!" she cried as I stuffed my feelings.

Woke around noon, alone in Rachel's bed. Outside the rain beat down, merciless as Genghis Khan after a four-month campaign on horseback before the invention of Preparation H. It had been a wonderful night, an eight-hour nude hugathon. Soft skin, full lips, fantasy breasts, hydraulic hips. Not to mention legs from Flatbush to Bangkok.

The note said she was at work, to have some of the still-hot coffee and let myself out with the extra set of keys. I drank a cup and smoked a cigarette. The apartment was pleasant, white walls and simple furniture. No pictures of Mommy and Daddy, no posters of idiot rock stars. No stinking cat or dying houseplants. It was calm and serene. So unlike the cluttered cribs of my bachelor-day pickups. I nosed around the closet. Roller skates, inversion boots, raincoats. I poured a big bowl of cereal for Natasha, and she chewed the fruited loops noisily. The HDA Program was working, truly working. My heart had wailed for what it had lost, but now my soul could laugh, for I had found so much: a beautiful new sex-addict girlfriend, a loyal loving pooch, good friends, money, an identity. I was the Scourge of Gotham City, the Crackerjack Exterminator. Big Jim and Farmer Rob had shown me the path, and I was walking the walk. Working the Steps. Sobriety was a wonderful journey, chock-full of surprises but no coincidences. As long as I trusted the process, followed God's will and not my own, things would turn out just fine.

I drank more coffee, smoked another cigarette. Breakfast of champions. Washed up. Drank more coffee, smoked another cigarette. The hard rain kept right on a-falling with biblical ferocity. I studied the bundle of heroin I'd copped at the bodega. For the old Ed, this would have been a perfect get-high day. I'd snort a few bags for that sweet instant jolt, the bitter opiated drip drip drip down the throat, the immediate sense of security, the absence of care and blockage of worry, the beautiful warm flower blooming in my chest, blossoming in my veins, blanketing my body with poppied peace. I'd listen to the rain and let my mind wander. But hey, I didn't need that anymore, I was living life on life's terms, had my head screwed on straight and was chasing the middle-class American dream of contentment.

I stubbed out my cigarette. Time for work. Had to get back on the case, find my sons, take that Fourth Step, the complete and brave moral inventory of my life, peel the smelly layers of the onion, expose my character defects, resentments, anger. I had to discover and nurture that glorious flower within.

I called Myron at the office.

"Is this my favorite sponsor?"

"That you, Ed?"

"C'est moi, chérie."

"You're cheerful and talking French. To what do I owe the pleasure?"

"It works! It truly works!"

"You got your kids back?"

"Not yet, but I'm working on it. Myron, I'm in love."

"You slept with the dog?"

"Myron, Myron, your mind works in mysterious ways. I spent the night with Rachel from The Program."

He clucked. "Not good."

"Not good? Do you have any idea how long it's been? I thought you'd be happy for me."

"She's working the Thirteenth Step on you. Seducing a newcomer. That's a no-no. You're not supposed to have a relationship for your first year clean. Start with a plant, and if that lives you get a pet, and if that lives you get a relationship."

"Don't be so old-fashioned."

"I'm being a good sponsor. You gotta trust the process."

"Okay, how's this? I was a vegetable and I lived, so I got a dog and she's living, so now I have a girlfriend. Case closed."

"Ed, your sobriety is your life. You have a fatal disease. A disease which tells you you don't have a disease. Anything which threatens your life is my concern. As Farmer Rob said, 'Behind every skirt there's a slip.' Slip means relapse. S-L-I-P: Sobriety Loses Its Priority. You might have another binge in you, but do you have another recovery? Besides that, she's unstable."

"And what are you? The Rockette of Gibraltar?"

"We're not talking about me, wisenheimer. My mental

health or sex life is not the issue here. If you really need
to know, I happen to be celibate. I overdosed on sex before
I came into The Program."

"Well, I underdosed. I was a deprived husband. One
of the *New York Times* hundred neediest cases. Rachel is
God's gift."

"You heard her share?"

"Myron, did she ever share! All night long!"

"At the meetings, idiot. Ed, I've been listening to her
wacko life for three years now. You don't need it. Her
ex-significant other is a crazy guy, jealous too, a coke
dealer. He's out there — on a major-league run. I suggest
you tell her you love your wife and then avoid her like
the plague."

"You're telling me to lie? I thought this was a program
of rigorous honesty. I just want to be happy."

"Yesterday you loved your wife. Today you're com-
mitting adultery. You don't know what you want."

"No, Myron, Michelle is dead to me. I'm a widower.
By accepting reality I feel free."

"Big Jim said, 'Feelings aren't facts.' Your thinking is
stinking. Admit it: you're in denial. You love her. Michelle is alive and sick. She needs help."

"Let her go to Hookers Anonymous."

"You're such a goddamn smartass. Why don't you ask
your Higher Power to remove that defect?"

"What, and walk around naked? See you later,
Myron."

"Easy does it, Ed."

The cold rain tattooed my head, soaked my hair, weighed
my longcoat down, liquefied my socks and sneakers to

lead heaviness. Natasha peed, then squat-thrusted steaming golden nuggets. We set off crosstown, puddlejogging.

Whatever else, my dead wife was a good mother. She
wouldn't neglect the boys' education. Why hadn't I
thought of checking their school? Myron told me that
first night that newly sober brains take a long time to
clear up. "Five years to get your marbles back, and then
another five years to learn how to play with them." Fuck
that shit — my mind was hitting on all cylinders.

I tied Natasha to a parking meter and let her sit there
with her lamb, forlorn in the cold rain.

"Sorry, babydoll; I'll be back soon."

The security guard stopped me.

"I'm looking for Ms. Gonzalez's class," I said. "My
boys are Mutt and Jeff T——. Their mother died."

"I'm awful sorry." The old codger doffed his cap.
"That's room 303. Take the stairs."

It smelled just like the schools I'd gone to. The stench
of little-kid piss from the bathrooms blended with the
heavy institutional odor of disinfectant. Clammy and
warm, with hissing radiators. A place where dreams and
hopes could be fostered and fed. Wait till the little suckers
got out there in the real deal and tried to dip their meathooks into the diminishing stewpot of the world's bounty.
They'd find out; and when they'd been burnt enough
times, their dreams mashed to slime, then it would be
back to the stink of piss and disinfectant, only their new
holding pens, the hospitals, jails, morgues, and booby
hatches, wouldn't be nearly so friendly.

I hated school. I quit after my father bought the farm.
Maybe the disease was genetic. And dear old do-nothing

Mom, in the nursing joint, the homecoming queen at Alzheimer State.

I trudged the steps, sneakers squishing wet and loud. The third-floor walls decorated by the plump-lettered scripts of handwriting-contest winners and the cubist crayon drawings of elementary school Picassos.

303.

"Yes?" asked Ms. Gonzalez. I scoped the room.

"Sorry to disturb. I'm Ed T——. I don't see my sons, Matthew and Jeffrey."

"Children, be good," she ordered, coming out into the hall and closing the door on the instant hubbub.

"I've been worried about them lately." Large brown eyes behind gold-rim glasses probed my face.

"I just got out of the hospital," I told her. "And now my wife is very sick. She's got a terminal disease."

Her eyes popped wide in wonder and her pretty young face sagged with sorrow.

"I'm so sad to hear that."

"God's will, Ms. Gonzalez. God's will. Acceptance is the key. I'm very worried about the boys."

"This is their first day absent, but the last week they have been strange. Not at all their usual selves. I guess the stress of. . . . Why, Matthew insists his name is —"

"Donatello."

"Yes. . . . And they've always been sweet boys and almost, well, flirtatious, but now they're downright obscene."

"They both have serious crushes on you."

"I know; my fiancé loves the apples they bring." She showed me the small diamond glittering on her finger.

"Good luck, Ms. Gonzalez. Marriage is hard as a motherf. . . . Well, I wish you the best. It's not easy. My wife has kidnapped the boys."

"They're not with you?"

"Most certainly not."

"Then I will speak freely, Mr. T——. Yesterday Jeffrey's face was bruised."

"Bruised?"

"As if he'd been beaten."

The sickness came rolling over me.

"And I caught Donatello selling one of the other boys a video, *Doris Does Denver* — pornography. These are serious instances of child abuse."

"I had nothing to do with this. My wife is acting crazy these days and I don't know where they are."

"I saw her yesterday when she picked them up. I was looking out the window, keeping an eye on my car. Do you know how many batteries I've had stolen this year? Now I chain the hood. And hubcaps? I don't even bother replacing them anymore. And. . . . Anyway, when she picked them up she was all dressed up. . . ."

"Like a prostitute?"

"Yes! And the man with her, an African-American with a fancy car."

The class bell rang and the children streamed from the room like fresh-hatched smelts.

"Thank you, Ms. Gonzalez."

"Mr. T——, I've alerted the Child Welfare Administration. You can expect a visit. What else could I do?" She sighed apologetically. "Kids on drugs, kids with guns. Last week we caught a ten-year-old shooting heroin in the boys' room. They deal drugs on the premises, and every day we confiscate crack, pipes, beepers, knives, guns. Sir, it's a war zone. We've ordered a metal detector, but the Board of Education can't even afford new textbooks. Can you imagine what goes on in high school?"

Right then a black kid, no more than twelve years old, walked by wearing unlaced hundred-and-seventy-dollar Pump sneakers, a six-hundred-dollar fur-lined bomber jacket, and sunglasses. He was speaking on a cellular phone. "We outlawed beepers." She sighed again. "But now they have portable phones. It's a nightmare."

Leaving the school I felt like horseshit. It only got worse. Now Michelle had a pimp, a motherfucking pimp, and they were beating on my kids between fucks and sucks on the crackpipe. One day at a time it was a nightmare, a real live horrorshow nightmare.

Natasha sneezed. Poor thing, she needed hot food. What had she done to deserve this dog's life? Even though you couldn't rightly call hanging with Ed a Tupperware party or a church social, anything was better than being chained to a radiator as Flaco's prisoner. At least with me she had the opportunity to walk and run, urinate and defecate out of doors, go to HDA meetings, feel The Program love, and chew the odd Doberman or Mets fan.

Farther west on Houston. Natasha's toy lamb lay sodden on the wet steps of the doorway we hung in. She wolfed the hot pastrami sandwich I'd copped at Katz's Deli. I smoked and drank a coffee, looked at the paper. The rain pelted parked cars, melted cardboard boxes to beige pukeslime. Ludlow Street junkies strutted to and from fixes. Reptile faces in the cold wet.

The fucking *Post*. No surprise: Leonard Lump still

stinking up the front page. Sarah Syrup, so sweet she made your teeth hurt, got pages four and five — incredible cheesecake stills from her exercise videos displaying her lethal frontal artillery. Her pastor down home in Little Oblivion called her "a fine Christian gal, never missed a Sunday in church and sang pretty as a nightingale. Smart as a whip too." Nelson Mandela on page seven, dignified and white-haired, smiling radiantly, fresh from twenty-seven years behind bars. Freedom for a nation versus the "alleged" marital infidelities of a single rich publicity glutton. No contest. Fuck the *Post*. And fuck Leonard Lump. His businessman belly would slice up clean and easy as a fat Butterball turkey on Thanksgiving Day. Who was he to rob me of my day in the sun? I deserved the cover, for Oscar, for Flaco, for Pencil Neck. Or give it to Mandela. Me or Mandela. Give it to a humanitarian. Anyone but Lump. The *Post* had their priorities screwed up. Hell, I'd been a good reporter, and they'd busted me down to covering supermarket openings. And Kenny, photographing giant squashes and homeless pets. What a waste of talent and time. Wait a sec, Ed, listen to yourself. Work that Fourth Step. Can you hear the resentment? You're pissing all over yourself. You've been angry and resentful your whole life, and you're still stewing in your own stinking juices. You resented your father for his violence, your mother for sticking to him like a wet noodle to a hot pan, the preppies of St. Dismas for fucking with you, your wife for denying you sex, your kids for needing food when you needed drugs, the *Post* for bouncing your sorry ass, Leonard Lump for having six billion dollars and Sarah Syrup. Ed, Ed, cool down. How can you possibly work a good Program if you get so riled up? Accept whatever's on your plate. Be humble. God's been preparing you for this special work for years. Just stay clean and keep on doing the right thing.

But hey, page eight, here was talent! Too Tall's tortured face and blood-pumping stub of wrist. Goddamn Kenny. Wasting no time. It was a fine picture, full of drama and emotion. Good work. If Leonard Lump was a star shining bright for all to see, then I was a black hole, an invisible mystery of nature, destroying any flotsam and jetsam unfortunate enough to wander into my orbit. Powerless? If that was powerless, then there's a whole lot of power in just being powerless.

All of a sudden I felt sick. I burped mustard and bile, and the single bite of pastrami I'd managed to get down shot up my throat into my mouth. I spat it out. Christ, if Kenny sold them that picture, what was stopping him from selling them another, one featuring me? And where was the film being developed?

Right then the little kid I'd spotted speaking on the portable phone at school walked by on Houston Street, dry and warm as fresh unbuttered toast under a red-and-white-striped golf umbrella. I wiped mustard off Natasha's snout, shoved her lamb in her teeth, and swung in, half a block back.

I was ten feet behind when he stopped to hit a bell on an Alphabet City tenement.

"Yo?" came the intercom voice.

"Beam me up, Scotty," he squeaked, taking off his shades. "It's Wonder Bread."

The door buzzed open, and as he stood there closing his umbrella, I slid in.

He dished me fish-eye.

"You're home a little early from school," I said, neighborly.

"I be sick," he mumbled.

Natasha and I took the stairs slowly. Wonder Bread passed us on the third-floor landing, regal as Leonard Lump at a board meeting, giving wide berth as if we smelled, as if our poverty was contagious.

On the fifth floor he knocked on an armored door. I fumbled with my keys and made like I was going home.

"Wonder Bread," he announced, loud and proud. The door swung open and he sauntered in.

The whole setup gave me bad vibes.

I sat on the top step stroking Natasha, watching the rain through the broken stairwell window, thinking about all Ms. Gonzalez had said. I felt ill.

He was out in three minutes, swaggering past us like he just got laid. He stuck his tongue out at me. I stood up.

"Oh, Wonder Bread."

"How you know my name, ol' man?"

"You're a celebrity on the Peewee Crack League." I grabbed his arm. Natasha nuzzled his crotch.

"Yo, keep Spuds off me, man."

"Empty your pockets, punk."

"Fock that bo'shit, homeboy."

"Pleased to meet you too, I'm sure." I let go his arm and pinched his cheek hard, then gave him a bird's-eye view of my Rambo pigsticker. "I eat baby crackerjacks for breakfast. Empty them."

"You crazy."

"It's very possible," I said, smiling and pulling out

my Glock. "How 'bout you, shortstop? You packing?"

His eyes went small and angry, and he reached for his pocket.

"Easy does it." I touched the knife-point to his throat.

Gently, very gently, he produced a nine-millimeter. I went over to the broken window and flipped the gun out.

"Damn!" whined Wonder Bread.

"Now complete the inventory," I said. "Empty them."

The cellular phone, a plastic bag packed with full crack vials, seven hundred dollars cash, a Tootsie Pop, and his shades. I pocketed the money, put the shades on, and drooled over the coke.

Say, Ed, send the little gangster on his merry way and have yourself a nice little party. You could tear through a hundred bottles of rock in a few hours. Then go to a meeting, start a fresh day count.

"My posse hear 'bout this, you be toast."

"Sonny, one day you'll thank me for this." I gave him back his Tootsie Pop. "Keep the candy, snotnose, but remember to brush."

"Mafocka!"

"Leave my mother out of this." I pulled his ear. This little fuck was dealing to kids Mutt and Jeff's age. I shoved him to a sitting position on the steps, pulled his shades off my face, and dropped them down the stairwell.

"Those be Oakleys!" he wailed.

"Off with the Reeboks, knucklehead." I smashed the phone into junk.

"Yo, man, that be my phone!"

"Was your phone. Off with the sneakers."

"What you want with my Pumps, man? They ain't gonna fit yo' big ol' clubfeet."

I stabbed them with my blade. The air wheezed out and he groaned.

"Now the coat."

His eyes pooled with tears as he handed it over.

"Cost me six hundred fifty-nine dollar."

I slashed the brown leather.

"With or without tax?" I tossed the coat to Natasha, and she started whipping it around, pawing it, ripping it to shreds. "Pants and shirt."

He was crying now, as I made rags of his clothes.

I looked at his school ID.

"Okeydoke, Clarence." Now just a scared little boy weeping away, naked and shivering but for his Jockey shorts, socks, and three gold chains. "Give up the gold."

He groaned and passed the chains.

"C'mere," I said, sitting.

I bent him over my knee and spanked hard, the blows echoing in the drafty stairwell.

"Repeat after me: Crack is wack."

"Crack be wack."

"With more feeling." I spanked.

"Crack be wack!"

"Scotty is dotty."

"That's stupid."

"Say it!"

"Scotty be dotty."

"I'm out of business. Say it."

He said it, sobbing.

"Now, Clarence, here's ten bucks. Take a cab home

and tell your mother what happened. She'll understand."

"She gonna whup my ass too."

"Only because she loves you." I wiped his tear-stained
face. "Forget this drug shit, kiddo. It's nowhere. Save
yourself and everyone who loves you a lot of pain. The
war is over and you lost. Wonder Bread is retired. You
dig?"

"But I be plannin' to go to Harvard an' buy a Rolex."

"You keep this up, you'll be dead before you get hair
under your arms."

"You the man?"

"Clarence." I gave him a good look at my gun. "You're
looking at the only law in Crack City."

He sniffled.

"Don't forget your umbrella." Nice kid, I thought, as
he ran downstairs in his socks and shorts, sucking on his
Tootsie Pop. I hope he doesn't catch a cold.

I banged on the door.

"Yo?"

"Wonder Bread!" I cried in falsetto.

The door opened on — I shot him once in the
head — a stringbean Hispanic in tank top and shorts.
He clawed air and crumpled to the floor, spazzed out a
bit and lay there. Natasha dropped Larry Lamb and
licked the small dark entry hole in his forehead.

I closed the door softly.

Loud salsa pounded from a boom box. I scouted the
joint.

A *Town & Country* showcase it wasn't. The place was
littered with crackstems and crack. Ziploc bags full of

vials, empty and full, a fortune on the street. I changed the hyper Latin music to FMU and hummed along to "I Wanna Be an Anarchist." And then I smelled it, the familiar bittersweet odor of cooking coke.

A cold sweat broke on my forehead. I checked the bathroom. Empty. Closet. Nada. One door more.

I stood to the side, then slowly turned the handle.

An explosion. The door splintered to kindling.

I faked a pitiful moan.

The woman came out of the room with shotgun smoking, saw Natasha lapping at the dead man's puddled brains, then loosed an anguished scream.

I poked the Glock into her ear, took her shotgun.

She looked at me, hatred twisting her face, then spat. The thick oyster thwapped my cheek and slid down onto my collar. I put the shotgun down, wiped off, then punched her hard in the mouth.

"Asshole," I said, unclenching my fist.

Her lips leaked blood and swelled fast.

"Where's the cash?"

She swore at me in Spanish.

I walked her through the ruined door, into the other room.

"Well well well. What have we here?" The setup was impressive. "A goddamn crack factory." A huge caldron of cokewater was bubbling on a stove, steam pulled out the window by a fan. A couple of bricks of coke, and next to them ten boxes of baking soda — plus a box of rat poison to make it extra kicky.

"A regular cottage industry."

"Chinga tu madre."

"Leave my mother out of it."

Another Ziploc, this one fat with money.

"Look, Poppy," she said in perfect English. "We be partners." She grabbed my crotch, massaged me. "You and me forever. I treat you nice."

"Take your own inventory, bitch." I knocked her hand off.

"Hunh?" Her eyebrows screwed themselves into question marks, then she grinned, licked her bloody puffy lips, darted her tongue invitingly, threw back her mane of long black hair.

"You a mean one, Poppy. Maybe you wanna spank me."

"Maybe I do. Why'd you shoot?"

"The music, Poppy. Enrique wouldn't be caught dead listening to that shit." She cupped a breast. "Mira, big boy, you wanna smoke before we fuck?"

No, I didn't want to smoke, and I wasn't taking any prisoners either. I thumped her over the head with the blackjack. She went limp in my arms. The cokesmell was making me sick. I put my gun and sap away, leaned her over the hot stove and shoved her head into the boiling water, strangling her thin neck. She started flailing, but I held her strong and pressed her body with my own, my groin stirring to life against her bouncy little ass, the water scalding my hands and wrists — held her there and choked her neck until she quit struggling. Her thick black hair fanned out in the turbulent white water, soft and pliant, undulating like seaweed in the waves.

I let go and grabbed the bag full of dollars.

Natasha followed my command and laid off the brain

soup, picked up Larry Lamb and followed me out the apartment, up the stairs, onto the roof.

And as we traversed the rooftops in the sheeting rain, sirens sounding below, all I could think was: What a waste. With hair like that she could have done shampoo commercials.

Back home later that afternoon, I was happy to let Kenny up.

"What happened to Lassie?" he asked, pushing a fat brown dreadlock out of his eye, smoking and sweating and scratching as I bathed the Doberman cuts on top of Natasha's bruised knotted skull with warm soapy water.

"Dogfight," I mumbled around the Vaselined Q-Tip stuck in my mouth, like a cut-man between rounds of a prizefight.

"She's tough as a motherfucker; but she don't look so fresh."

"You should see the other dog," I said. "Natasha's my good girl." I stroked her flanks. "Loyal too. Not like some two-legged bitches I know."

"Uh, Ed, you got any spare bread?"

"There's a loaf of pumpernickel in the fridge." I painted the furrowed slashes with petroleum jelly.

"Yo, funnyman, I mean cashish."

"Take your coat off, Ken. Have a seat." I blew on the wounds. I didn't feel any too friendly toward my old pal. "I know what you mean."

"Then why you bustin' my chops?" He wiped a sheen

of drug sweat from his frowning brow, picked a patch of pimples on his neck. "You of all people can dig what a serious jones feels like."

"You shouldn't have sold that picture to the *Post*." I released Natasha and she trotted off to drink water from her bowl. I poured us each a cup of coffee and lit a cigarette.

"Yo, I made peanuts." He squeezed a drug pimple on his jaw with his fingernails, appraised the pus and blood, then wiped it on his pants leg. "How much you think they'd pay for the action shots with Natasha? Or the ones with you?"

"You threatening me?"

"No way, José; but look, I settled for chump change." He coughed. "So c'mon, bro, lay me onto some large green. I only got twenty bucks for those rings and I've already smoked two yards' worth today. Please, man, hook me up. I spent my last on some mighty fine jumbo and now I need a bag of D. Got a hungry monkey to feed who ain't heard nothing 'bout no Slim Fast plan."

"You deserve a break today." I fished the bundle of dope from my coat pocket and let him have a panoramic view of it. "Brandname McDonald's. Tell me where the negatives are and you win what's behind the golden arches."

"Yo!" he cried, sweating and shivering. "I got them."

"Who developed them?" I asked, cold and Gestapo-like.

"I did, man. At home. You think I'd send something that sensitive out?" He shivered again. "Ed, be a bro. I'm sick, really dopesick."

"You heard about that case in Georgia where a guy's

pit bull killed a kid and he got convicted of murder?"

He shook his head no.

"It was in the *Post* last month," I said, dangling the dope, watching him lick white crust off his lips. He was utterly hypnotized by the little swinging bags, and like a sleepwalker, he worked a hand under his shirt, into his pants, and came up with an envelope. I reached for it, opened it. They were all there, strips of evidence, yesterday's news. I felt better already.

"Knock yourself out." I tossed him the heroin.

"Yess!" he cried, like Marv Albert, the sportscaster, at a particularly lovely score. "My savior!" He came and hugged me. He smelled like death eating an onion.

He ripped a bag, put it to his schnoz and hoovered.

"Ahh." He sighed, slumping in a chair, veiny stem-scarred hands hanging loose, face easing up, licking his sore lips. "That's the real thang!" He sniffled. "Make me forget about my crack thumb." He held his swollen beaming thumb up for inspection.

I stared out the streaked window onto the Bowery. The windshield washers, put out of work by the rain, just begged.

"You see the cover of the *Post* today?" I asked.

"Motherfucking Leonard Lump." He contemplated his thumb.

"He's a piece of shit."

"Piece of shit." He nodded, rubbed his nose, then ripped open another bag and power-snorted. "You read where they're gonna drop caterpillars onto Colombia from airplanes to chew up the coca crop?" Kenny licked his thumb. "Page twenty-three."

"Is that so?" Pretty fucking comic. Me and five billion caterpillars fighting the war on drugs.

"People be snorting bugs and bugging out." He scratched his thighs. "Hey, that dope's good. Got a nice bitter taste."

"How's the book?" I asked.

"It's gonna be def! I met a fifteen-year-old Dominican crackwhore this morning, eight months pregnant. Wanted to nasty for ten bucks, said she'd lick my woody for three. I gave her twenty, just took pictures."

"You're a true gentleman."

"Nah, Ed, I'm a true fisherman. I already got a bad case of crabs." He scratched his crotch, sniffed. He really did smell. Like twelve-day-old gerbil shit. "Fucking crackbabies being born all deformed and addicted, with IQs lower than squirrels. The mothers still in junior high. Yo, Crack City is way-out insane. I need a vacation, bro, maybe quit jammin' and slammin' with Scotty."

"That shit makes you stupid, Kenny. It's Colombian roulette. You have two choices: change or die."

"Yeah, but how do I kick?" He bit a callus on his thumb. "I don't know if I could face withdrawal. Ten years ago I was on the methadone maintenance program and that didn't work for shit."

"It's not meant to. Adolf Hitler's science boys invented methadone so his morphine-addicted troops wouldn't nod out on the job. The 'done is the government's way of keeping junkies half dead. Just alive enough to keep buying cigarettes. The tobacco companies run this country."

"Yeah, and the multinationals and the CIA and the

Medellín cartel are all in bed together, having a ménage à fucking trois on a bedful of dirty cash. So what's a motherfucker to do?"

"Join HDA and become a Moonie like me. It's free."

"What do you do? Sit around talking shit and boo-hoo-hooing all day and night?"

"No, man. It's half group therapy and half spiritual growth. We get in touch with our Higher Power and work on our anger. We learn how to forgive ourselves for all the misery we've caused." I smiled. "We accept things."

"Yo, Reverend, you accept collect calls?"

"We accept who we are and what we were. F'rinstance, I have to accept having hit my wife."

He slapped his forehead. "I knew there was something I forgot. I caught up with Michelle last night."

"I saw her too. She stiffed me."

"Word. She split with some brother in a BMW. Soon's she got in the Beamer she beamed up. Don't take offense, Ed, but your wife's a stemsucking ho'." It was true, goddammit. No matter how sick it made me feel, I had to accept it. "I followed them in a taxi. Got an address for you."

I already had my coat half on. "Why didn't you say so?"

"Don't get pissed," he said, sucking his thumb and scratching his balls. "The crack's done rotted my brain." He forked over a slip of paper with an address, then hit his knees and searched the floor carefully, as if he'd dropped a contact lens. "Yesss!" he cried happily, pulling a stem from his pocket. "I'm just a partying Cossack!"

he announced proudly, kneeling like he was in church and stuffing the stem. "Beam me up, Scotty." He flicked his Bic and sucked. "Yecchh." He spat, disgusted. "Fucking plaster."

Ah well, if Kenny wasn't yet ready for the twentieth-century miracle of recovery, he might as well get high. So I handed over Clarence's bag of rock. "Crack it up," I said and left him sitting on the floor, smiling like a well-fed Buddha, flexing his thumb.

THE years of wear and tear had made us stupid, one day at a time. Life was not a bowl of cherries; it was a plateful of pigshit.

I cabbed it through the rain over to the address Ken gave me, a brownstone on East Thirty-fifth. Rang buzzers one by one. Two women, one old man with Italian accent, three zips, and then, with the name Washington, paydirt.

"Hello?" came a child's voice. A pang of adrenaline shot through me. It was Mutt.

"Special delivery," I said.

The door buzzed. I shouldered it open, took the carpeted stairs three at a time, and reached the apartment huffing.

I knocked.

The door sesameed open and I barreled in. Mutt's eyes bugged.

"Where are they?" I asked, pulling the Glock, looking for the pimp.

He whistled. "Bitchin' gun, dude. Totally awesome."

I tore all over the plush ultramodern pad, with big-screen TV and stereo, checked the bedrooms off the main living-kitchen area. Mutt was alone.

"Yo, homeboy, wanna beer?" he called from the refrigerator.

"No." I sank into a soft sofa. "I'm clean now. Where's your mother?"

"Out with Jeff. How was Detroit?"

"I was in detox, not Detroit." It seemed a million years ago. "Where's the scumsucker?"

"Jeff's out with Mom."

"Where's Washington, smartass?"

"On the dollar bill."

"The guy who lives here."

"Uncle Trust? Mom's friend? His name is Trust."

Mutt sat across from me in an easy chair, holding a sweating red-white-blue can.

"What are you doing?" I asked.

"What does it look like? Havin' a cold one. Cowabunga, dude, this Bud's for me."

"You're eleven years old." I took the beer and poured it into a tall potted plant. "Are you fucking crazy, Mutt?"

I looked at him, and it was like looking in a Twilight Zone mirror. Same blond crew cut, same fuck-you sneer. This was a nightmare.

"Yo, don't call me Mutt. I ain't no mongrel dog. I'm Donatello. Who the hell are you?"

"The proud father of a mutant turtle."

"Yo, I'm cool." He tied an Oriental headband around his head. "Get with it, dude."

"Look, Matthew, I'm your dad, not your dude, and don't keep saying 'yo.' "

"Yo, what's wrong with 'yo'?"

"It's drug talk."

"Yo, what's wrong with drugs?"

I went to the window and looked down on the traffic crawling through the rain across Thirty-fifth Street.

"Drugs are death. I've been down that road and I hate what I became."

"Don't get sappy on me, dude." He was silent a second, then said, "Beam me up, Scotty."

I turned from the gray day, and there was my little boy, his lips wrapped around the glass dick, sucking flame, puffing hard on a white rock. A fucking prepubescent crackerjack.

I went and yanked the pipe from his mouth.

"Yo!" He laughed, blowing honeysuckle-sweet coke-smoke on me. "If you wanted a hit, you could ask."

I dropped the stem on the floor and ground it to powder. God, the crack smelled great.

"Since when are you a crackhead?"

"Suck my dick," he said, reaching for the remote control and zapping the video on. I raised my hand to swat the foul-mouthed pest.

"What? You gonna hit me too? Mom was right, you're a fuckin' maniac."

"Don't you know that crack kills?"

"Hey, old-timer, you're still alive, and I seen you beamin' up like Captain Kirk. Like father, like son. Anyway, all the dudes in school smoke." The wall-sized screen was filled with the image of two naked blond women rubbing and licking, oohing and ahhing. I was shaking I was so pissed. Easy does it.

"Relax, dude, uh, Dad. Like check out this radical lezbo action. Tiffany be home soon."

"Your mother's name is Michelle and this is not your home."

I flicked the remote off.

"Don't have a cow, man. Check out this gnarly TV. Mom told us this is our home. You think we want to go back to that shithole downtown after livin' here? Dude, Scotty's really got your number. Hey, Uncle Trust promised me and Jeff Pump sneakers. Then we be ultra-bad, like the def dudes in school. Besides, Mom's callin' the shots. She's got a new waitress job and gets lots of tips. So take a chill pill, Oprah's comin' on."

"Mutt —"

"Donatello."

"Matthew, you think this is a big joke?" I lifted my leg and stomped a sneaker through the glass coffee table. The glass shattered to shards with a reassuring sound. "Where's the Trust?"

"Fuck if I know."

"Where's your mother and Jeff?" I swept books from a shelf.

"The hospital. Jeff's face is fucked up. Chill out. You got an extra cigarette?"

"Stop clowning." I looked around for something to destroy. "What happened to his face?"

"He got a bitchin' shiner. Word up, dude, you are kinda old — how 'bout Donahue?"

"Your mother hit him?" I gripped him hard by the arm.

"Hell no, he slipped," Mutt whined. "Let go, that hurts." I dropped his stick of an arm.

135

"Hey, man," he said, boldness returning. "Gimme a Marlboro."

"He slipped?"

"That's the story. Hey, ya wanna watch 'America's Most Wanted'? Uncle Trust taped it."

"You hit your brother?"

"Don't say nothin'. Uncle Trust really popped him good for mouthin' off last night. Mom was at work."

"He hit Jeff."

"Don't say nothin'." He pouted. "Uncle Trust got a nasty temper. The first time he backhanded him, I took the rap. But last night he went nuts. Look, he told us it wouldn't happen again, and if we didn't rat we could have all the rock we wanted. He's gonna give us jobs too."

"Let's go." I grabbed him by the collar. "Lace your fucking sneakers. We're getting out of here."

"Keep your pants on, dude. Let's order a pizza and watch Geraldo."

Natasha licked the last of Mutt's vomit from the floor of Frank's car.

"Bad girl," I said and wiped up with paper towels, chucked them out as Frank gassed up at the Hess filling station on Tenth Avenue. We'd just put Mutt on a Greyhound to Detroit. It had been a busy few hours. Back at my place: cigarettes, coffee, and phone calls, then — driving through traffic and rain to the bus station.

First I'd called Frank. Sure, he said, he'd be happy to give us a ride. Then Michelle rang up in a panic over the missing Mutt. I told her Trust had whacked Jeff, that I was sending Mutt to her folks. She confronted Jeff right then. He admitted the real deal and Michelle announced she was leaving Trust. Not coming home (I asked), anything but that — she was going solo. Then I called Ma and Pa Kawalski. Horrified by the tale of Michelle's bellyflop into the dark side, they agreed to take the crackerjack kid, promised to get him some therapy and take him to church.

Driving through the wet foggy night, Mutt prattled on: Trust Washington, Teenage Mutant Ninja Turtles, the pornographic wonders of Hyapatia Lee, the glories

137

of crack. He denied a problem, claimed he was a normal fifth grader with normal interests, and incessantly begged for cigarettes. Frank gave him a lit Camel and he puked his guts out. We put him on the bus, sick and coughing. There'd been an unpleasant moment in the station when he saw the butt of Frank's revolver, asked to see it, and after Frank refused, snottily said, "I bet my old man's piece is bigger than yours."

"I think I love her, Frank." We were back in traffic, smoking cigs.

"You really got your nose open for that crazy Rachel?"

"Better than having it open for a bag of dope."

"What's the diff? Babes or bags, both big fuckin' trouble." He sighed. "Sounds like infatuation. This too shall fuckin' pass."

"Sounds like you might be a little jealous, Frank."

"Jealous? Over a nutty fuckin' piece of ass you'll probably go out over? Shit, I give you three weeks tops before you're back suckin' Satan's shlong. You're gonna slip behind that skirt."

"Look, man, just 'cause I quit getting high doesn't mean I have to stop living. Myron told me The Program is a bridge back to life, not life itself. I don't plan to be one of those Moonie ostriches with their heads in the sand, spouting Farmer Rob and Big Jim sayings out their asses like a goddamn tape recorder."

"Easy fuckin' does it."

"There you go again. Stop with the slogans."

"What's your fuckin' problem, man? You want to work your own fuckin' Program?" His voice got loud and his eyes flashed cold. "What did the kid mean with that gun shit? You got a gun, Ed? You got a fuckin' piece?"

"What's the problem, Frank? You got a wild hair up your ass? Still playing cop?"

"I don't play at anything, Ed." His eyes probed. "You got a handgun?"

"Watch the road, Dick Tracy."

"Watch your mouth, crackerjack."

"Little testy, aren't we? Focus on yourself, junkie. You're on suspension."

Frank's right hand snaked toward his shoulder holster. He was fuming.

"I thought you had to hand in your gun, Frank."

"We're talking about you, numb-nuts. Your kid said you had a piece."

"The kid's been beaming up. That was Scotty talking."

"Izzat so?"

"I thought you and I were friends."

"Hey, pal, just 'cause I'm on suspension don't mean I ain't a cop," he snapped. "You don't fuckin' like it, you can walk." He paused and scratched his head. "Ed, I'm tryin' to fuckin' help you. You get caught with an unregistered handgun, you pull a year, automatic."

"Thanks for the concern, Frank, but you're not my sponsor."

Rain battered the Firebird windshield. The wipers snipped hypnotically. It was getting hot in there. Tension thick as cheese soup. The city a yellow rumbling monster. Neon lights refracting through the streaked windows like a rainbow with the spins. We smoked in silence.

"Look, Ed," Frank said with a sigh. "I don't mean to be an asshole; it just comes natural. I've been wanderin' in the woods for so fuckin' long, I can't expect to find my way out in an instant. I gotta give time time. Those fuckin' sayin's are a real comfort. I apologize for goin' off."

"Me too." Really, we were recovery brothers. It was God's will we remain friends. We shook.

"I had a shit day," Frank confessed. "The Department called me in and grilled me. They're lookin' for some fucker with a gripe against dealers. But they ain't lookin' real hard, if you know what I mean. Ballistics reports these fuckin' bacteria are gettin' wiped with a Glock. It's on record I used to own one. That was one sweet fuckin' piece. Traded it for heroin." He lit a Camel and blew smoke out his nose. "Y'know what's fuckin' hilarious about it? I'm a big fan of this dude. I mean, it goes against all my fuckin' cop trainin', but I hope he fuckin' makes it."

I had to strangle the urge to dish him the goods. After all, he bled NYPD blue.

"I hope he makes it too, bro," I said, my voice and emotions under control. "And if he doesn't" — I looked at him and smiled — "maybe you'll take over." We both laughed.

"What do you think about Leonard Lump?" I asked, to change the subject.

"Solid-gold piece of shit." Frank spat out the window. "You?"

"He's evil as any crack dealer out there. It's guys like him jacking up the rents and forcing people out onto the street. He's a bigtime scumsucker."

"Yeah, but how 'bout that Sarah fuckin' Syrup? I'd eat her till her head caved in." He lit a fresh Camel. "Ed, how did Natasha get those cuts?"

"She had a slip."

"You're fuckin' pitiful," Frank said, laughing, and gunned the car east into the bowels of Crack City.

"WHEN you feel like getting high — and you will feel like getting high — go to a meeting." I wanted that drink, every bone and particle in my body was screaming for it. Beer signs were flashing in my head, commercials blaring in my memory. The little devil disease had said its piece and the committee had voted for it unanimously. I'd hit a meeting later. I had to walk a bit, clear the cobwebs. I was powerless. Over everything.

I walked through the rain. Frank had gone to the HDA Center. I wanted to be alone.

"Who the fuck you think you are?" he'd asked. "Greta fuckin' Garbo?"

"I just need space to think."

"Stinkin' thinkin' leads to serious fuckin' drinkin'. Come to the fuckin' meetin' and arrest your goddamn disease. You got a case of terminal uniqueness."

"Don't feel like a meeting."

"That's when you need one most, numb-nuts. The self-pity is oozin' out your ass. As Farmer Rob said, 'Poor me poor me pour me a drink.' Easy fuckin' does it, Ed."

Sure, easy does it. I liked the rain. It made me feel clean. Walking the streets with Natasha made me feel strong, made me feel clear, made me feel sober. Take the action, let go of the result. I was getting good at that.

There are no coincidences in HDA, and it was no coincidence that a chipmunk-cheeked crackerjack beaming up in a doorway on Tenth between B and C caught my eye.

"Yo, how mehee oo nee?" he asked, pocketing his stem, cracking his knuckles.

Aw, Christ, a crack dealer with a speech impediment. Poor fucker, the only place for him was the street, where the democracy of compulsion made everyone equal. The vulture was a victim and the victim a vulture. Eat and/or be eaten.

"Watchoo stain ak?"

"Ain't staring at shit," I said, moving on, sad for the mushmouth in the rain.

"Who fuck 'oo fink oo ah caw me shik?" he mumbled, on my heels.

"Take a chill pill, brother — you know what I mean."

"Don' caw me brovvah. Ah aintchoo brovvah."

He didn't understand. Didn't understand I was like him. I, too, was an outcast. But there was a solution.

"Hey, man, you want to come with me to a meeting? Free coffee?"

He moved toward me.

"Don't do this," I said, putting my hands up and backing off as he advanced, fitting a pair of brass knuckles.

Natasha growled around Larry Lamb. I held her close.

"Teace oo lesson." I pulled my head back and the brass fist grazed my cheek, sending signals of rage and pain to my brain.

I sidestepped, reached into my pocket and pulled the Glock. It all felt like an ugly acid trip déjà vu. I didn't want to, but there was no choice.

His armored hand was swinging again.

I was close enough to see grains of gold in his green eyes.

And I was sad sad sad as I shot him clean and accurate, once in the throat. He touched his neck delicately, reeled drunkenly, then folded up, rolling into the gutter. Blood jetted like a fancy fountain from the small hole. His head lolled, mouth opened, and he spat ten bloody crack vials like broken teeth into the streaming streetwater.

"Sonovabitch," he said, clear as a TV pitchman selling denture cream, and the nausea and coffee rose in my throat. "Tell my old lady I'll be late for dinner."

"SOBER," said the speaker on the podium, a small bald white man in priest get-up. "S-O-B-E-R: Son Of a Bitch, Everything's Real. As Big Jim used to say, 'My worst day sober is better than my best day drunk.' I believe that."

"What a crock of bullshit," I whispered to Rachel as I lit a cigarette and gulped a coffee. "That's the stupidest one yet. These Moonies can convince themselves of anything."

"Don't you like being clean?" she asked, taking my cold hand, which was raw and hurt something fierce from the scalding water I'd shampooed the girl's hair with yea those many centuries ago that afternoon.

"Sometimes it feels dirty."

"Thanks a lot," she said, insulted, dropping my hand. "Feelings aren't facts. Put some gratitude in your attitude." I ran my unburned hand through her thick curls and massaged her neck.

"Sorry, Rachel. I didn't mean it that way."

She touched my cheek tenderly. "What happened to your face?"

"Cut myself shaving."

MICHAEL GUINZBURG

Natasha slept at my feet as we listened to the man spin his yarn.

"I was a whiskey priest, and I need to remind myself how bad it was and what can happen if I go out there again. I'm not worried about the yets: jails, mental hospitals, or death. I'm afraid of the agains: the madness, sadness, gloom and doom, the fear and futility of dancing with the disease. I may have another binge in me, but I don't believe I have another recovery."

Myron winked at me from across the room.

"As Farmer Rob said, 'Would you let others do to you what you have done to yourself?' Of course not, my friends. Many of you know me from the *Post*. My story was big news some months back."

Sure, it was Father Bryan, head of Calvary House, the nationwide shelter for teenage runaways.

"I have been accused of embezzling funds and engaging in sex with young boys. Perhaps I did these things. I don't remember. I'd never do them today. The last years of my drugging and drinking were one long blackout. I'd wake up in the morning, full of anxiety, throw up into a bucket by my bed, and then get crocked again. I had to drink a bottle of wine, then vomit it up, just to get the first vodka down. My choice of drugs was drugs. Pills, liquor, cocaine, opiates — these were my friends, my allies, what I needed to function. Coke allowed me to drink more. I banged heroin in the confessional. Did speedballs before mass. Quaaludes for christenings. You name it. And booze always. More times than I care to remember I crapped my pants while giving a sermon. I had rubber sheets on my bed. I even jumped out the window, broke every bone in my body, but still I drank.

I justified it by saying if God wanted me to quit, He'd have allowed me to die. I wasn't yet sick and tired of being sick and tired. I hung around chickenhawk bars, after-hours clubs, S and M discos. I was your best friend until your money or your drugs ran out. Then I ran out. At an ecumenical conference, I kept going into the bathroom to sniff coke and drink moonshine from a flask I stashed beneath my robes. I'd take water in my mouth and spurt it into the toilet so the other priests would think I was urinating. My flock wondered why I wore sunglasses all the time, even at night; but you all know. How many pairs of Ray-Bans did I lose? I was in detoxes, rehabs, private clinics for priests, and I never got the message. I made the pilgrimage to Farmer Rob's barn. I tried geographic cures, went to Santa Fe, Milwaukee, New Orleans, all over this country. I went to Europe, Australia, Asia, South America. I dropped in on meetings all over the globe, listened to the Twelve Steps in foreign languages I couldn't even speak — and let me tell you, The Program love is the same whatever the tongue — but I never truly surrendered. I was still Father Bryan, shepherd of the downtrodden, a willful egotist, the great I AM. I stuffed my real feelings. My emotions were numb. I was spiritually dead. Farmer Rob wrote that ego, E-G-O, means Easing God Out, and that was what I was doing. I couldn't admit then that God works through people, that this Group Of Druggies is G-O-D in action. 'We can do what I cannot.'

"I was a sinner, but sin has led me to salvation. I hated myself, but now I love myself. Like Shakespeare's King Lear, I'd say, 'Out, out, vile jelly!' — in hope that my obsession to get high would be lifted, that the insanity, which I then didn't realize was a disease, would be purged from my body. Big Jim defined insanity as 'Doing something over and over and expecting a different result.' I had a compulsion of the mind, an allergy of the body, a sickness of the spirit."

I sat straight up in my chair. Father Bryan spoke directly to my heart, defining my addiction, holding a mirror up to my disease. I ID'd with him, word for blessed word, right down the fucking line.

"That vile jelly I so wanted plucked from me is what the Eastern sages call the third eye of the mystical body, the organ of spiritual vision and illumination. The disease brought me to my knees before my God. Like Big Jim Williams, I, too, had a spiritual awakening. We have all read about Big Jim's white light, the feeling of peace and serenity he experienced when, still withdrawing from alcohol and morphine, wrestling a large Frenchman in Des Moines, Iowa, he was pinned to the canvas and saw the light, the beneficent white light of God's love, when he surrendered, finally surrendered to his powerlessness and, in so doing, to his Higher Power, and then got sober. I had a similar illumination. I was with some of my runaways on a fishing trip. I had been partying heavily, drinking, eating Valium, Seconal, and Percodan like they were breath mints — my tolerance was sky-high. I was coming off my crush-and-shoot phase. I'd crush pills, especially Dilaudid, and shoot them. Sometimes I shot vodka, or just water, to get the feel of the needle. That day the boat ran into something and sank. Everyone but me had a life preserver. I was caught up in the fishermen's nets. I was stoned out and under water, drowning, struggling to free myself. The more I struggled, the more entangled I became. Then I heard a voice and saw a light, and the voice said, 'Bryan, quit struggling.' So I stopped flailing, became very relaxed, and the nets untangled. I'd let go and let God. You see, I did have a life preserver, my Higher Power, whom I choose to call God. I floated to the surface, free of my obsession to get high. The misery was over. I have never gotten high or drunk again. But I know if I took one single drink I'd be right back where I left off, moments from death. That's the way the disease is — it's progressive. And make no mistake, it wants us all dead.

"In a way, I love this disease, for it has allowed me to find the rooms of HDA, to know God's love. Addicts are special people. God protects us while we are in the throes of active use, then leads us to the salvation of recovery, to the healing shelter of institutions, to the grace of death. Hallelujah, I say unto you, there is no stigma in addiction! I'm proud to be an addict, proud to carry the message of Hard Drugs Anonymous, to serve God. The great psychiatrist Carl Jung praised the healing powers of our Fellowship. He understood that the strength of the collective unconscious is right here, and it's the only effective remedy for our brand of spiritual bankruptcy. If God takes away my collar, if God sends me to jail or the mental hospital, I won't complain. You see, I am a happy man now that I'm not doing it my way. My way was madness. Now I do it your way, the clean and sober way. Your way is God's way. God's way mends my sick and suffering spirit. One day at a time, I come to meetings and arrest my disease. I feel my feelings. I love you all and thank you for my recovery."

It made my heart soar like a B-52 to see someone

else whose life was crumbling but who hadn't lost faith.

They passed the basket and did the usual drill of anniversaries and under ninety days. Again, it was thrilling to hear the people applaud for me. But as I looked around at all the happy faces, it dawned: they weren't cheering and grinning for me — not for the real Ed; they were clapping for someone else, that sensitive fellow who'd lost his wife and kids and was trying to get sober. I felt empty. I didn't belong.

"My name is Arnold, and I'm an alcoholic and addict."

"Hi, Arnold!"

"I'm back to day one again. Last night I shot dope, and I felt like I wanted to die. They say The Program ruins your drinking and drugging. It's true. I felt dirty. I know why I got baked. I was feeling sorry for myself. I wanted to stuff that feeling. So I medicated myself. The problem is that the feeling was magnified. I was thinking about my life back on the farm in Wisconsin, how my family was so screwed up. A dysfunctional family, my sponsor says. My mother never wanted me. In fact, she didn't even know she was pregnant until she was rushed to the hospital. See, she weighed over three hundred pounds and suspected she had a tumor. I was that tumor. She used to joke about it to her friends in front of me. Called me her tumor baby. . . ."

Arnold sobbed. His jowls jiggled like jello on a roller coaster. The kid was so damned honest. He put me to shame.

"No wonder I stayed fucked up. Low self-esteem. Last night after I got off, I only felt worse. I don't recommend it to anyone. It's the loneliest feeling in the world. Without you people, I think I'd commit suicide."

"Thanks for sharing, Arnold." Father Bryan beamed beatifically. "Keep coming back. Pain is the touchstone of spirituality. Don't stuff it, let it out. You're God's beloved child. He truly loves you. God is good."

"My name is Frank, and I'm a fuckin' drug addict and alcoholic."

"Hi, Frank."

"You were a fuckin' nutjob, Father, but I admire you breakin' out of your fuckin' hell and I ID with screwin' up on the job — though the only fuckin' twelve year old I ever gobbled was a fuckin' bottle of Wild Turkey. Me, I'm a cop, and right now I'm on fuckin' suspension 'cause of my drinkin' and druggin'. And let me tell you, it sucks. But even so, I just can't stop thinkin' like a cop. Even here in the meetin's. I imagine you shitbirds going out on binges and knockin' old ladies over the head for their purses. And worse. And I see myself doin' wild shit, pluggin' dope dealers and whatnot. I know it's a sick fantasy. I'm mixin' up who I was with who I'm fuckin' becomin'. Why be a paranoid fuck? That was the old Frank. The new Frank doesn't fuckin' care if you boink your sister. Oh, guess fuckin' what? I finally made a friend here in The Program. That's progress. Right? I really get off on helpin' someone else get sober." Frank smiled at me. "But my fantasy life is so fuckin' bizarre — I see my buddy doin' crazy shit."

I felt a cold shudder wiggle my spine.

"Carin' is responsibility, and I don't know my limits. I gotta learn limits. In the old days I didn't have limits. You fucked with Frank, you ended up in the hospital, at best. I was outside the law, outside reason, but I ain't goin' back there. It was a cold and ugly place, and I was one mean, suspicious bastard. I really ID with you. When I switched from booze to heroin it was like goin' from the *Titanic* to the fuckin' space shuttle *Challenger*. Sure, drinkin' sucks, but sometimes I say fuckit, I'm not an alcoholic anymore. I'm cured. Wouldn't a cold fuckin' beer taste good?"

The priest laughed. "Frank, remember what Farmer Rob said: 'Once a pickle, never a cucumber.' God is good."

It was fine and dandy for Father Bryan to be amused by Frank's ranting, but I was chilled to the bone. I couldn't look at him. The hardness in his voice was bad enough. Fuckit, even if he knew, he didn't have proof. No one had proof. And he was right. A cold beer would taste good.

"My name is Luis, alcohol and drugs."

"Loo! Loo! Loo!"

"You people are beautiful. Yesterday I got my ninety. I felt like a kid on his birthday. I'm so happy to be clean. No more dopefiending or basing it up, and I don't got to wear no sunglasses at night no more! Three months ago I was a thief. I would go into these sneaker stores, tie up the dudes working, and then fill a garbage bag full of Air Jordans and Pumps and then sell them uptown for fifty bucks a pair. I didn't hurt no one, but now I read where kids are dusting each other for sneakers, and I don't feel so hot. So maybe I gets me a job working with kids and that'll be my Ninth Step amend. I got a lot of work to do on myself. I come from one of them dysfunctional families too. Everybody was always dissing everybody, but thanks to The Program I'm a clean serene love machine, all because you people loved me when I couldn't love myself. Thanks."

"We still love you, Loo. God is good. And there is room in His heart for everyone."

Oh really? How 'bout for an ex-reporter with a smoking Glock and a collection of bodies?

"My name is Rachel, and I'm a drug addict and alcoholic and a sleazy slimy sex addict."

"Hi, Rachel!" cried the sober mob, and I felt my face go red as the room shifted its ravenous gaze upon my cherished chick.

"I'm an actress, and today my agent called and told me I had the lead in a beer commercial. I turned it down. I'm waiting to see if I got this soap opera. I can't sell alcohol with my face or body. Booze is a lethal poison. What if I influenced children to drink? That's a form of child abuse. I was an abused child and I wouldn't wish that kind of hell on anyone. I remember what Farmer Rob said: 'Alcohol preserves that which is dead and kills that which is alive.' I did this detergent commercial last year and had spaghetti spilled on my lap, and that was okay, but beer! No way. I love acting so much. And I owe any chance I have for a career to staying clean in HDA. When I was getting wired, doing cocaine, I didn't study my lines, I snorted them.

"I really identify with all your sexual acting out in blackouts. Thank God I don't recall half the things I did. You should have seen some of the guys I woke up with. One man was so hairy I thought he was wearing a gorilla suit. Really. It's a wonder I didn't get AIDS. My ex-significant other, who's relapsing, called me at work today and he wants a reconciliation. I said, 'No dice. You took advantage of me, and now I'm seeing someone else.' He cursed me out and I'm really scared of him. He's got a real nasty streak."

"Stick close to the rooms, Rachel." Father Bryan flashed the pearly whites that had made him a Casanova on the chickenhawk circuit. "Don't jeopardize your sobriety. That's why we call it a selfish program. You're no good to anyone unless you stay sober. God is good."

The meeting dragged on and on. I didn't feel like talking. I felt like splitting. There were places to go and people to see, old debts to settle, amends to make. I had to work The Program, had to work it fast, and I had to work it clean. No more lunacy. I had to find Jeff. If Michelle really had ditched Trust Washington, where would she go? And Kenny — the pictures. Yeah, I had the negatives, but what if he'd made prints? He could still sell them to the *Post* or the cops. And Frank — what if he knew? What would he do about it?

After the prayer, men hugged men, women hugged women; pensioners in JCPenney ensembles glued nicotined lips to the soft cheeks of teenage girl addicts; rich women in fur coats clinched with homeless men in rags; a redheaded preppy girl mashed faces with a nose-ringed black skinhead. There was something truly beautiful about it, like a revival meeting. Hope was in the air.

I lit a smoke. It tasted dead and sour, like powdered tooth off the dentist's drill.

Rachel looked at me with love in her eyes.

"Let's go for coffee," she said.

"Sure, but I need to see my sponsor a minute."

"Meet me at the Kiev," she said, kissing me lightly

on the cheek. "I'm going to the corner to call mine." I watched her rumpswing her way out and up the stairs.

"Let's go for coffee," said Frank.

"Can't. I need to talk with Myron."

"What happened to your face?"

"I gave myself a home lobotomy."

"Real fuckin' cute, Ed," he said sarcastically. "You wanna tell me what really went down or do I gotta ask Natasha?"

"I met this nearsighted vampire."

"Ed, I'm your friend. When you feel like cuttin' the crap and talkin' honestly, gimme a fuckin' call. You got my number." He gave me a look of utter disgust and stormed out.

Myron looked splendid in his peasant skirt and hoop earrings. The white ruffled shirt offset his black hair. The faint smell of Obsession accompanied his bearhug.

"What happened to your face?"

"I haven't mastered the fork."

"Ed, get serious."

"Okay, Myron, how's this? I got one of the boys back."

"You see, it works, it truly works!"

"He's a crackfreak. I have to accept it, so I sent him to the in-laws in Michigan." I took a heavy suck off the rancid Marlboro. "Myron, I need to do a Fifth Step. Will you hear my confession?"

"Ed, you haven't done the first four yet. There's a procedure to it. You need to write them down. Look, we have all the time in the world to work the Steps. Just stay clean, honeypie, and we'll do them. Trust the process."

"Myron, I have writer's block and I can't wait. I gotta work the Steps. I need to confess. It's God's will I confess. I have feelings eating me up inside."

He sighed, wrote his address on a scrap of paper.

"Come by later. I'll take a bubble bath and brew some coffee."

SOME nights when you're bone-tired and feeling stupid and stinking from all the hard years of drugging and drinking and the events of your life are reaming you up the ass and the only thing that might make you feel comfortable in your skin is making a deal with Scotty and beaming up a nice boulder of cocaine hearing that glorious crackle like bacon sizzling in the pan spattering your brain with the sweet grease of relief or smoking a mm-mm-good-tasting fat joint of Hawaiian or chipping away on some nice China White heroin or all of the above or maybe just guzzling fifteen or sixteen cocktails like everybody's all-American — just escaping from your shit for a little breath of time and wiping out the nightmare of history — but getting high isn't an option anymore: all you can do is buy another pack of coffin nails and go for coffee. Some fucking nights you just feel like dying.

You walk through the misty East Village with your loyal dog — your wife is a whore and your kids are crack-heads — and you hate everybody you see — crackerjacks and beggars and yuppies and vendors and junkies and Germans and smiling ponytailed pseudo-artists — one with a sweatshirt that says "I shop therefore I am" —

and all the happy young couples in love spilling from the bars walking hand in hand making plans for tomorrow for the weekend for the next fifty-five and a half years — and everything bothers you burns you up is a personal insult and this living for today shit is making you crazy . . . you just gotta keep it simple and jam another clip in your gun and walk the walk 'cause however much you want out of Crack City and to be done with the circus of killing you know in your heart-of-darkness heart it's not over yet and why would you want it over it feels so good so damn good so powerful so sweet so goddamn godlike and maybe those preppies who'd grow up to be yuppies were on the money you're a bloodsucking leech and maybe too that shrink back then was right — maybe it's a helluva lot simpler than all that constant wondering wondering what's it all about Alfie — maybe you just plain hate yourself. Well, fuck him too.

Rachel waiting. Rachel sitting there lovely enough to eat. Rachel with radiant face full of hope. Rachel, sweet Rachel, in black boots and tight black jeans and black leather jacket, tight white T-shirt with black Botticelli curls. Rachel.

"Coffee and a cheeseburger for me," I told the roly-poly Polish waitress.

"I'd like a mushroom omelet and fries and a large cherry Coke, please," said my darling sex addict. "Ed, I feel marvelous, like I was reborn. Last night was really special." She took my hand, stroked the smarting flesh, and shyly said, "I love you."

I stared out the window at Natasha tied to a parking meter, nuzzling Larry Lamb.

"Easy does it, Rachel." I took my hand back and lit a cig. "I dig you too, but I'm married, I have two kids — and the future? I can't project about the future."

"Who said you could? Love is like sobriety: take it one day at a time." Rachel got up. "Excuse me a minute. I have to use the powder room."

My hand ached. My cheek stung. Fatigue throbbed behind my eyes like an exaggerated aspirin commercial. I shut them. Put my fingers in my ears to keep from hearing all the depressed, out-of-work actors discussing their nowhere careers. They came from all over, bursting with impossible ambitions, from every jerkwater East Bumfuck in America, came with stars and dollars signs in their eyes, and New York chewed them up and spat them out old and tired and disillusioned, with excellent typing skills and bad livers. I was tired. Jesus, was I tired.

"How was work?" I asked as Rachel sat, feeling almost married to this bizarre beautiful stranger.

"Oh, just a regular day at the office. One guy wanted me to pee on him — that's extra. Another had me dress as a nurse. And this rich dude from Utah tipped me a hundred bucks. So dinner's on me."

Our food arrived.

"What'd you have to do for the hundred?"

"Nothing too complicated." She slathered her eggs and potatoes with ketchup, red red ketchup. "He dresses up in a crotchless Batman uniform." She set to chomping her food with gusto. "I whip him, paddle him, spit on him, y'know, generally give him pleasure. Call him every disgusting thing in the book." She guzzled soda. I left my burger alone and lit another smoke. "His time is almost up, and he shows me pictures of his wife and nine

159

kids — he's a Mormon — and then he looks at me with these puppy-dog eyes and begs in this little baby voice, 'Kick me, Mommy, kick me where it counts.' I'm wearing these pointed boots with steel toes, and he's got this really big old hard-on . . . what's the matter Ed, you not hungry?"

"Finish the story."

"Okay," she said, a forkful of fries poised at her sweet mouth. "He says, 'Pretty please, with sugar on top?' So I haul off and boot him one in the nuts, and guess what?"

"What?"

"He shoots his wad." She chewed her food and chased it down with soda.

"I really hope you get that soap opera role." I lit a fresh smoke and looked out the window at a wino puking in the gutter.

She finished her food and stared at my burger.

"So do I. I mean, I do like my work, but acting is my passion. God, I'm nervous. With you in my life and the possibility of getting the part, I really really feel like my plate is full. Ed?" Her eyes gleamed. "If you don't want your burger, may I have it?"

"Go for it."

"Hey." She laughed, pouring ketchup while I downed the last of my coffee. "Nothing like a hard day's work to build up an appetite."

"Rachel, I got one of my boys back today."

"You see, it works, it truly works. That's wonderful!"

"I sent him to my in-laws till I get my life under control. You know how shitty it feels to admit you can't take care of your kids?"

"Don't beat yourself up about it. It's a selfish program.

160

'Anyone or anything that jeopardizes your recovery must be cut from your life like a tumor.' I quote Big Jim."

I stubbed out my cigarette.

"My wife needs help."

"The hooker?" She chewed, ketchup dribbling from the corner of her mouth. I wiped it with my napkin.

"The mother of my children."

"The sleazy slimy bitch."

"She's sick, Rachel."

"I'll say she is. Out screwing strangers for money, with AIDS all over the place. Skipping out on you when you were in the hospital recovering from a fatal illness. You don't think she's a bitch?"

A vision of detox danced in my head. The paper gowns; the piles of bland food; the hopeless old-timers with their oozing-sore-carpeted stick legs, bloated feet, and scabby leather faces, just resting up for the next joust with the bottle; the fiending crackerjacks screaming and moaning in their sleep — and me, helpless and hallucinating rats everywhere, sweating and shivering and feeling like a zombie, just one more of Scotty's mutant crackslaves.

"Waitress!" called Rachel.

"Where's your compassion? Michelle is an addict. She has the same disease that we have. That your ex-boyfriend has. Do you hate him?"

"I'll say I do. He raped me." The waitress stood poised with pencil and pad, oblivious to anything but items on the menu. "I'll have a strawberry shortcake, extra whipped cream, and nuts, lots of nuts. Oh, and half a cantaloupe. Ed?"

"Coffee." I looked out the window at Natasha, lying

low, ears flat, little hooded eyes watching me through the window. Christ, she was sweet, loyal, uncomplicated.

"He was straight a long time and then he got high. Now he's out there dealing drugs again. He came over to get his shit last week and he forced me to have sex with him. I'm not the forgiving type, Ed. That's one of the defects I choose to hold on to. It's a selfish program. Take the best and leave the rest."

"What's the scumsucker's name?" A knot in my belly, and it wasn't coffee.

"Shorty."

"Where does he operate?"

"Why? You're going to beat him up?" She laughed, as if me fucking with Shorty was an unlikely idea. And then her face grew serious. "Sometimes I think I'd be better off as a lesbian. Men are such dickheads."

Dessert arrived. She started in demolishing her cake. I sipped the scalding black java, sparked a Marlboro.

"Rachel, I got you a gift." I handed her the gold chains I'd snatched from Clarence.

"I love them!" She put them on. "Thanks." She leaned across the table and planted a whipped cream kiss on my lips. "Oh boy, wait till I tell my psychiatrist about this!"

"Seeing a shrink helps?"

"How do you think I've gotten so much better? He's the only man I trust." She went to work on her cantaloupe.

"You don't trust me?"

"I don't really know you, Ed. The fact that I love you makes trusting you that much harder. It started with my father. I wasn't in touch with this stuff before I got into therapy. Hypnosis has been really useful. Now I'm aware of my dependency issues and I don't stuff the feelings. I accept them. Waitress! A slice of cherry cheesecake. Where was I? Oh yeah, my father. I loved him so much. He was an artist, a very handsome man. He painted while my mother worked. I'd cry and cry and not even a bottle helped, so he set my crib by his easel and, well, he would unzip his pants and let me use his penis as a pacifier. That stopped the crying. One day my mother came home early from work and saw what we were doing and she went after him with a kitchen knife. I watched this from my crib, crying and crying. Daddy turned the knife on Mommy and he cut her throat. She died. He went to prison. I went to the orphanage."

"That's where the food thing started?"

"Uh huh." She scooped cheesecake into her mouth, barely chewing, just swallowing the red-and-white mush. "I really missed my father. I couldn't forgive him for leaving me. Thank God I don't have an eating disorder now."

"Rachel, you just put away enough to feed a family of four."

"That's because I'm hungry, silly. If I had a problem with food I'd know it. I'd admit it. And for sure I wouldn't be willing to share. Here, have some of my cake."

"No thanks." I felt ill.

"Sweetie, would you excuse me a moment? I need to use the little girls' room. Don't worry about the food; it's under control."

She ran for the ladies' room. I heard her wretched retching and a torrent into the toilet. Then a flush.

She returned to the table and wiped her lips. I took her hand.

"And you know what, Ed?" I raised my eyebrows. "When I turned eighteen I went and read the transcript of the trial. The cops found his pubic hair on my mouth."

I felt nauseous. "Let's pay the check," I said.

"Waitress!" Rachel signaled.

I really needed some air.

"Waitress," said Rachel, "I'd like a mushroom omelet and fries and a large cherry Coke, please. Ed?"

"Just coffee."

DROPPED Rachel off at her place, left Natasha, said I'd be back soon, had to square an old debt. After all, cleaning up the wreckage of the past was part of The Program.

Igor and Ivan, obese middle-aged Ukrainians, made and sold kielbasa in their home. You don't get rich selling sausage from your sofa, so to pay for their summer house on the Jersey shore, the brothers had a sideline: they were merchants of high-quality coke and dope, catering to the Eastern European émigré addict set.

"Hallo, Ett," greeted Igor, huge and blond, seated on a reinforced steel chair in his kitchen, wearing a tank top and boxer shorts, watching "Lifestyles of the Rich and Famous." He was one fat fuck, a four hundred pounder, a cigarette stuck in the corner of his mouth, chopping away with a bloody Ginsu knife at a variety of raw meat, pig hearts, chicken gizzards and kidneys, beef liver, sheep guts, calf brains. He shoved guts into a huge meat grinder next to him on the counter, stubbed his red-soaked cig out, then popped a bloody kidney in his mouth.

"Lonk time no see." He chewed around his thick accent, blood staining his lips.

"I owe you a hundred," I said and peeled him the bread.

"Yah." He wiped his bloody hands on a towel, pocketed the green, then took a straw and snorted a long line from a mirror, half brown, half pink, a gourmet speedball. His blond-lashed pink eyelids fluttered.

"Dot's goot," he said. "Wot I ken do for you?"

"Where's Ivan?"

"He not feelingk so goot."

"What's his beef?"

"Ha!" He giggled; his bulk jiggled. "Dot's fonny! Hees bif! Ivan hass proplaam breedingk. Assma dey call eet." He razor-chopped a pink rock, spread it, then postscripted it with a tail of brown powder from another pile. "Thees vary goot sheet. You try."

The sweat popped out on my hairline, the queasy feeling took over my stomach. Robin Leach sang the praises of a luxury New Mexico health spa, "where the spiritually minded jet set take mud baths and get in touch with their past lives."

"No thanks, Igor. I just came by to pay you guys. I quit getting high." Damn, it looked delicious.

"You kweet?" Spasms of laughter rippled his blob. "Ett, you mekk beeg joke. You keedingk. Thees ees goot brown heroin from Goldten Triankle and peenk flekk coke from Payroo. Ees byuttful. Try eet, you lak eet." Igor threw half a calf brain over his shoulder into the corner. A fat gray rat poked its nose from a hole in the wall to grab the meat. "Rot ees shy. Doss not know he ees pet."

"Igor, my friend, I better leave." If you drop by a barbershop, you'll end up with a haircut. The coke and dope looked so fine, why not take a sniff? Why not buy a whole shitload, stay high for the rest of the century? Why not just cut my balls off and feed them to the rats? "I have to split."

"Ett, tekk a cheel peel. Go say hallo to Ivan. He ask alwess, whar Ett ees?"

I made my way back to Ivan's bedroom, sweat drenching my underarms, legs wobbly.

"Ett!" wheezed Ivan from his bed. He was wearing a Members Only T-shirt and he too was watching "Lifestyles." A big grin creased his wart-speckled pink face. He pressed a button and the Craftmatic adjustable bed whirred, raised his massive body to a lounging position. He proffered a hamhock hand to shake. "Luke at thees! Shoorly Mugglain ees een mod bat, spikkingk een voice of Egyptian pharaoh!"

It was true. The actress was neck-deep in mud, chattering away about the pyramids in a baritone voice.

On the night table: a few ounces of bagged brown heroin, flanked by a few ounces of sparkling pink coke, a scale, a roll of tinfoil, and a box of Baggies. My salivary glands pumped overtime.

"You want spidball, Ett?" Ivan's blue eyes smiling in friendship, pupils pinpricked by the dope.

"Ivan, I just came by to say hi, pay you the hundred."

"Not to worry abott money, Ett. You are frand. You hongry, you want kielbasa?"

"Ivan, I quit getting high. I feel better. I want you and Igor to come with me to a meeting, this Twelve Step group I go to. Free coffee."

"Ett, I no dreenk coffee. Ees bat for you. I no go nowhar. I no kweet drogs. Ees only theenk mekk my laff okay. You no want gat high, you no gat high. Me, I gat high. Ees goot. Eef goot, no rizzon stop."

"No reason? It's the plague, it's living death, it's stupid and selfish and there's no glamour in it. I say this as a friend, Ivan. You're wasting your life."

"Ees my laff! Frand no tal frand wot do!"

"Ivan, you have a serious problem. Come to the meeting. You can talk about your childhood, get in touch with the feelings."

"Now you mek me matt. Thees ees free conetree. I want forgatt chaldhoot. Stalin keel avverbotty."

"Let me fluff your pillow," I said. What the hell was I doing there, trying to carry the message of HDA?

"Ees okay." His face was not happy. He stuck a large reefer in his mouth and lit it. The pungent smell of Thai weed drifted over and taunted my nostrils. "Ett, you smoke."

"I stopped getting high." Lord, I wanted to smoke, wanted to fit my lips around the warm spicy herbstick and suck the sweet smoke of life into my dead soul.

"Ha! You sweatingk. You misserubble. Smoke and tekk a cheel peel. Forgat proplaam."

The herb smelled fantastic, transcendent, out of this world. Why would it be growing wild all over the planet if it wasn't good for you? The Rastas use it as a sacrament. But wait, if you abuse a sacrament it stops being holy, it becomes evil. Ivan was tempting my disease. In league with Scotty. What would Big Jim say? "Anyone or anything that threatens your recovery must be cut from your life like a tumor."

"Ever see one of these?" I pulled my gun.

"Yah, ees Glock weet silencer. Vary nice. You want

tredd?" He blew a smoke ring at me. It exploded in my face, and the rich reefer aroma said, "Baby, I love you; come home to Mama."

"Ivan, put the joint out."

"Ees free conetree. You no frand."

"Just a fucking customer? Put the joint out."

"No tal me wot do een my house! Liff now, Ett."

"Where's the cash?" I put the gun to his head, turned the bedside TV's volume up.

Robin Leach's voice was brutally loud.

"Een frizzer." His pale-blue eyes were moist with fear. "Pliz, Ett, I bag you. No do thees."

"Don't beg, Ivan, it's disgusting."

"I bag you. I go to meetingk. I bag."

"Beggars can't be choosers."

He pressed his hands together in prayer. That game wasn't working. I had no sympathy for the devil. An outhouse stink rose from his shorts, masked the pleasant Thai weed smell.

"Too little too late," I said and, feeling happy, joyous and free, shot him four times in the chest. Ivan's soft mass jerked orgasmically. He wheezed and moaned, burped some blood. A yellow stain spread his shorts. Red colored his Members Only-logoed chest. I picked the bag of heroin up and emptied it onto his punctured front.

"I'm not a bad person, Ivan, just kind of sick." His wounds absorbed the dope with a wet sucking sound. He trembled and wheezed and then was still. His eyes stared blue as robin's eggs at the ceiling. He looked damned peaceful. I'll bet he'd forgotten all about Stalin.

In the kitchen, Igor sat transfixed by the television.

"How Ivan ees?" he asked.

"Ivan's got the farts."

Igor laughed. "Poor sonvabeetch."

"Yeah, but I think I cured his breathing problem."

Robin Leach droned on: "Missouri megabillionaire Stan Dalton discovered that in the seventh century he was a pregnant seven-year-old peasant girl in rural France who died in childbirth. Acting upon this information, he built an abortion clinic in Marseilles. . . ."

Igor laughed, sniffed a line, pushed the mirror toward me with a broad smile.

I had no choice. Igor had to go. I bopped him behind the ear with my blackjack and he tumbled, sweeping bloody animal parts off the counter, and when he thudded, the floor rattled. I put the gun to his little pink white-haired ear and pressed the trigger. The sweet ffftt noise, and he flopped about like a fish out of water, then just lay there, a bloated blond whale of a man with blood draining in a slow trickle out his head.

I opened the freezer and plucked packs of rubber-banded bills, took a pint of Oreo Crunch ice cream, and from the fridge a bag full of packaged kielbasa, then grabbed a spoon and set to eating ice cream. As I left, a few rats were already coming out of the wall to feast on the scattered inner organs, and Robin Leach, always a stickler for etiquette, was MC'ing the banquet.

"Ed, sweetheart, what's the matter?" Rachel clicked her light on, sat up in bed and rubbed her eyes. Natasha sniffed the bag of sausage and drooled.

"Nothing," I said, taking off my coat, tearing open the bag for the pooch. "You look beautiful."

"Nothing? You're crying. Come to Mama. What's wrong?"

"I don't know." I laid my wet face against her cool white breasts. Oh, but I did know. My wife was a hooker. My kids were crackheads. I'd just killed two friends. The pressure in my head was unbearable.

"Baby, it's okay." She smoothed my hair. "Early sobriety is a bitch. It gets better."

"Rachel, I'm so confused."

"You're still detoxing from the drugs. When I got clean I was insane for months. I couldn't sleep or eat and I was so shy I couldn't share at meetings. At least you're dumping your shit, Ed. You're not holding back. I really admire that."

"There's something I need to share, Rachel. I just . . ."

"Yes?" She was so delicious, so innocent-looking, I just couldn't tell her.

"You want some ice cream?"

"Oh, Ed, the very idea makes me sick. I'm really embarrassed about that display I put on tonight. You see how bad the disease of addiction can get? While I was in the food, I was totally denying I had a problem. I'm glad you're here. I was having a nightmare about eating, sex, and my father."

"I'm sorry."

"Don't be. You didn't do anything."

Natasha noisily gobbled kielbasa.

"I wish I'd been here. Maybe you wouldn't have had that bad dream."

"Don't beat yourself up about it," she said and unzipped my fly. "You're here now, Daddy, and you brought dessert."

I couldn't fall asleep. I kept thinking about Igor and Ivan, the mushmouth in the rain, the bodega dude, the Hispanic couple, Too Tall, Oscar, Pencil Neck, Flaco. Ten dead. All fucking dead 'cause Ed was getting sober. Drug dealers are bad, they spread filth and misery, but who was I to take anyone else's inventory?

I got up and carried the phone into the bathroom.

"Myron, I'm sorry to wake you."

"That's what I'm here for. You coming up?"

"I'm sorry I missed our appointment."

"Don't beat yourself up about it. Are you sober?"

"Of course."

"Then you have nothing to be sorry about. What's the matter?"

"I'm such a fuckup."

"Ed, don't beat yourself up. You're a good man. Is it Rachel?"

"No. Yes. Myron, I love her. But who'm I kidding? I still love my wife. I don't know. I don't know shit. I've been acting out and . . . "

"Keep it simple, stupid. Get some sleep, then come over for breakfast. I'll make pancakes. I'll even take the day off from work. Okay?"

"Sure."

"Who loves you, Ed?"

"I don't know. Who loves me?"

"Myron does, silly."

Still, I couldn't sleep. Every time I closed my eyes I saw red. I know it sounds goofy and phony and clichéd, but all I could think about was blood, rivers of blood and oozing brains. I had to stop beating myself up about it all. Had to accept the truth and deal with it. Okay, okay, so God wanted me to kill, to show the children that drugs don't pay off; but that didn't mean I had to feel good about it, that didn't mean I couldn't stop.

Back in the bathroom, I looked up the Self Help Warehouse, a twenty-four-hour hot line and referral service listing the Twelve Step groups of the tristate area. I'd seen it advertised on late-night TV back when I zoned out to the stain-remover ads, the Hair Club for Men show, the cellulite cream hour, and all the rest of the sad late-night rip-off programs for unhappy insomniacs.

"Self Help Warehouse, good morning. How may I help you?"

"Hello," I said. "I need some information. I'm trying to hook up with a support group to get my feelings out about a problem I have."

"Sir, you have to be more specific. We have Twelve Step groups for many disorders. Is this a compulsive thing?"

"It sure is. Will you tell me some of the groups?"

"Are you an alcoholic or a drug addict?"

"I'm already in Hard Drugs Anonymous."

"Are you an overeater? A gambler? A debtor?"

"Keep going."

"Kleptomaniac? Heart attack sufferer? Concentration camp survivor? Scared of crowds, of heights? A geriatric virgin? Are you addicted to any particular color? Automobile addict? Chocoholic? Compulsive jogger?"

"Worse."

"Are you a gay fundamentalist?"

"Please, lady, it's bad, really bad."

"Manic-depressive? Compulsive shopper? Are you a man who loves women who love too much?"

"What the hell is that?"

"If you have to ask, you're probably not one. Are you a trichotillomaniac."

"I don't know what that is."

"Someone who pulls their hair out."

"I might be if I don't get some help."

"Sir, give me a hint. It can't be so bad."

"It is."

"Well . . ." She sighed. "Are you addicted to newspapers? Television? Masturbation? Widower? Recently divorced Catholic? Jew who eats ham? Vietnam vet? Lower-back pain? Married cross-dresser?"

"Not even close."

"Look, sir, we list Twelve Step programs for most every obsessive-compulsive disorder you can think of. I myself am cross-addicted, a manic-depressive overeater alcoholic Jew who eats ham. What's your problem?

"Lady, have you got a program for murderers?"

"Yeah, it's called the federal penitentiary."

"I'm serious."

"So am I."

"No Twelve Step program for brutal killers?"

"Is this a joke?"

"No, ma'am. I need help. I'm responsible for ten deaths this week, and I'm not sure I can stop."

"Sir, I advise you to get a lawyer, stand in front of your local police station, take twelve steps into the building, and surrender."

Early morning. I kissed Rachel's warm belly, smiled at her pleasured sleepsigh, then dressed.

"Where you going, sweetie?" she asked snoozily, eyes behind a screen of black curls.

"To Myron's, to do my Fifth Step."

"Mmm. I hope you put your demons to rest."

Delancey Street. The sun breaking orange over the rim of Brooklyn. Natasha peeing an endless stream. Early cars and trucks rolling off the Williamsburg Bridge. I took a deep breath. Air so cold, clean, and clear. Natasha so happy, joyous and free, with her little lamb friend held gently in her jaws. Garbage whipping in the wind. Broken glass sparkling. It was good to be alive.

Myron answered the door in a white robe and pink bunny rabbit slippers, his face tired and showing age without makeup.

"Hi, Ed." He yawned, kissed my cheek. "Let me brew some coffee."

"Don't go to any trouble."

"Nothing but the best for my pigeon."

He brewed the java, washed up, put some soft classical

music on the stereo. His place was humble, clean, very feminine.

"Who's that — your father?" I pointed at a gold-framed photo of a thin jug-eared man with white hair and a look of extreme kindness and serenity, wearing bib overalls.

"Heavens no. I'm from the Bronx. How many Jews from Walton Avenue you know wear overalls?" He giggled. "That's Farmer Rob."

I sat in a chair. Myron brought forth a steaming mug of fresh coffee and a bowl of water for Natasha. I lit a cigarette.

I pointed to another photo, this one of a heavyset man in sweat clothes. "That your dad?"

"Sorry, Ed. That's Big Jim Williams. You might say Rob and Jim are my spiritual fathers. They gave me a blueprint for living that I never got at home."

As Myron went about whipping up fresh pancakes, I told him my story, how as kids my friends and I would burn ants with a magnifying glass under the sun, how my old man controlled me, how anytime I cried he threatened to send me to "Crybaby Farm" (where "crybabies from all over the globe sit around bawlin' like a buncha candy-ass fairies"; at the first sign of tears, he'd pick up the phone and dial a number, ask if they had "a bed and a box of Kleenex for a little girl named Ed"), how he beat the old lady, how he wouldn't let her show me affection ("Don't pamper him! You want him to be a sicko?"), how I got into drugs — most of the rage, pain, hatred, humiliation, and resentment of my childhood, crowned by what happened in the woods at St. Dismas.

"Ouch," he commiserated, a syrup-dripping forkful of flapjack near his mouth. "That must have hurt. No wonder you turned to drugs." Myron chewed. "So let me get this straight: your father never caught you in your Vietcong costume?"

"Umm. Yeah, he did; but I don't think I want to talk about it."

"Ed, you can't flush this stuff away unless you clear the pipes. This is a program of rigorous honesty. We're only as sick as our secrets. Come clean."

"Okay. It's like this. Ma was off visiting her father, and Pop came home completely stinko. Saw me dressed up and torturing a G.I. Joe, and he lost it. Tied me buck-naked to the radiator. Beat me and kicked me. Over and over. And that's not all he did, Myron. After he polished off another fifth of Seagram's and watched two John Wayne flicks on the tube, he bent me over and . . . how can I say this politely?"

"Just say it."

"He enlarged my asshole."

"Ouch!" He sipped coffee. "I know the feeling."

"He called me his little geisha girl, his Saigon whore. He pissed in my straw coolie hat. I lay there bleeding, and he laughed. Gave me a shot of whiskey and raped me again. He fed me bread and water and gave me a bucket to go to the bathroom in. This went on for a couple days. I guess he was in a blackout." I pushed my plate of pancakes aside. "When Ma came home she freaked. And when Grandpa died, she shipped me off to St. Dismas. One year later, the summer after prep school, Pop was dead, the old-fashioned way. He chowed down on his own pistol. My mother cried for a solid month, but I sure as hell didn't. I was relieved. I went wild, became a serious junkie. Stealing, running with dopefiends and whores and . . ."

"Tell me," he said, calm and priestlike.

"Well . . ." My appetite returned, and I stuffed my mouth. "I've got a lot of weird feelings about my part-time job after I quit school. I told my mother it was a grocery store in the Bronx, and she was cleaning rich people's houses so she never checked, but really I worked in a dopehouse, a shooting gallery. Helping junkies get off. Hey, these pancakes are outrageous."

"Thanks. What about the junkies?"

"Their hands would shake and their veins had no pressure, so it was up to me to hit them up. "Doctor, Doctor!" they used to call, and I'd run over to administer their shots. In the neck, between the toes, under their tongues, in their dicks, wherever I could find moving blood. I was good. I'd pull fluffs of cotton from my sweatsock to strain the shot so there were no air bubbles, and then I'd hit them. When the blood came up in the tool, they'd smile. That was part of the ritual. Show them their blood. Back then heroin was three bucks a pop, and I made bags or half bags as tips, then sold my extras for cash to take home to Ma." Myron coughed, and I drank coffee. "But now that I'm clean, I wonder if maybe one of the kids I turned on got a habit and died from it. Yeah, we all take our chances, but I still wonder."

"Ed, you were in the clutches of the disease. Pray for them, and for yourself."

"Man, I thought that was living. I was down for anything. Stealing, smoking dust, dropping acid, eating pills, doing whores, shoplifting, writing graffiti on subway

179

trains. One night my boys and I got into a spraypaint fight, and I came home all covered with red paint. Ma woke me for work and bugged. She thought it was blood. Guess she was flashing back to the old man. I had to calm her down so she could fix my eggs. I was there the night Tony La—— bugged out on angel dust and killed his mother with a steak knife. She gave him shit for coming home high. 'No, Tony, no!' she screamed in this Italian accent, but he was out of his tree, Myron, just kept on sticking her in the gut. Then he went into the living room and watched TV. Like nothing ever happened. I called the cops, and when they showed, Tony went after them, in hysterics, and they wasted him. The place was a fucking bloodbath. I was holding dust and heroin and a set of works. So Family Court sent me upstate to this psychiatric reform bin, where they shaved our heads and made us scrub toilets with a toothbrush; therapeutic duty they called it. I promised myself no more needles and narcotics, and I stuck to it. Still, we managed to stay fairly high, lots of pills and reefer and home-brewed rocket fuel. Did a year and a half and got sprung when I turned eighteen. Took a bus back to the city, got drunk as shit, and joined the navy. I considered pot, hash, and booze being straight."

"You tried to do it your way."

"My way. You know, Myron, every crummy bar in America has that Frank Snotrag song 'My Way' on the jukebox. I used to call it the loser's national anthem."

"Hey, Ed, many was the night I sat in my cardboard box guzzling gasoline and singing that tune. It was a great justification for self-pity."

"But my way used to work. The feeling you get when

you shoot a speedball, like you're God. The world takes on a beautiful glow, and when the coke kicks in, you feel fucking immortal. You ever see the tape of Elvis singing 'My Way' a few weeks before he croaked? Myron, it's incredible. Here's this fat twisted cartoon of Elvis, with drugsweat pouring out his face — I mean, you can see the toxins — and he's got a voice that makes Caruso sound like a mouse and you can feel he's a dead man, like his body is near dead, but he was never more alive, never, and the voice and —"

"Easy does it, Ed."

"But Myron, I feel like Elvis. Like I'm a dead man and my soul is flying. My way got me where I am. I think I'm still doing it my way. What I'm saying is that under all these layers of drugs and attitude I'm the same —"

"You're the same sweet boy who loved his mother and resented the hell out of his father."

"Myron, I'm the same violent fuck that . . . that . . ."

"Go on."

"In the navy they taught me how to use weapons and kick ass."

"Were you in the war?"

"Nah. I missed Vietnam. But hey, drug life is a war all its own."

"And nobody wins. Except the lucky ones who find The Program."

"I'll drink coffee to that." We clinked mugs. "Y'know, Myron, I always wanted to belong, to be a part of something. That's why I got high. In the junkie world we were all blood brothers and sisters. We shared. We were a community. Cocaine ruined all that. It makes people

181

greedy and selfish and evil — cocaine and now AIDS. These days, you share blood, you're a dead motherfucker."

Myron coughed. "Ed, if you hadn't gotten high you would have killed yourself, or maybe someone else. You would have been a sociopath. That wasn't a childhood you had; that was some kind of hell."

"You okay?" I asked, as he continued to cough.

"All this talk of blood makes me nervous, and when I'm nervous I cough. I'll be okay." He went off to the bathroom and came back with a bottle of nonalcoholic St. Joseph's cough syrup for children. I looked out the window. It was snowing.

"So far," he said, swigging orange syrup from the bottle, then staring at his pink slippers. "So far we have plenty of material for your Eighth and Ninth Steps. You'll make a list of all the people you harmed and resented, and then you'll ask their forgiveness."

"How about the ants?"

"I don't know, Ed; that's the least of your worries. Go to the park and leave bread crumbs. I meant your wife and kids, your mother and father, the preppy who ruptured you. The junkies? Pray for their souls and eventually, after you string together a couple of twenty-four hours, you'll do Twelfth Step work, spreading the message of HDA. It's a lifelong process. You never graduate from The Program."

I lit a cigarette. "Myron, I have secrets I need to share."

"That's what we're here for. We're only as sick as our secrets."

"I think I'm sicker."

"Ed, you gotta learn to wear your sobriety like a loose garment."

"My wife is a fucking addict, so are my kids, and my sobriety feels like a pair of underwear five sizes too small."

"For that you go to Junk-Anon."

"But I set the example. I was a hostile animal in my own home."

"Let's go back. How did you meet your wife?"

"She was dancing topless in the Lolita Lounge to pay for ballet lessons. We fell in love." Myron smiled and nodded as I told him about the good years, the kids, how we called our apartment the Little House on the Bowery, how I only smoked pot and drank beer, how happy and in love we were, how I went from copyboy to cub reporter, to reporter, then star reporter with an eye for hard news and biting commentary and an uncanny ability to talk to criminals. "Life was great."

"What happened?"

"Crack." I related my descent into the grease pit, the years with Scotty, ending with the peepshow, hitting my wife, detox.

"Live with the feelings. Accept them. And then forgive yourself. God surely has."

"I can't forgive myself." I sighed. "And I truly doubt that God has." I looked at the snow swirling thick outside. "Now I'm fucking crazy."

"Easy does it, Ed. The Second Step tells us that our Higher Power can restore us to sanity. Meditate and turn it over."

"Myron, I have blood on my hands."

"Wait a sec." He picked up the phone and called his job, told them he was sick. He sure sounded sick, hacking his lungs out. He took another pull of St. Joe's, refilled my coffee.

I took a deep breath, lit a cigarette, and filled him in about my busy week, all the way from Flaco to Igor and Ivan.

"At first it made me feel so good, but now —"

"Ed, you're not serious?"

"Oh, but I am, Myron. I tried to tell you before, after Flaco, but you wouldn't believe me. You read the *Post*." I pulled out the gun, the knife, the blackjack. "There are no coincidences in HDA. Serious? I'm deadly serious."

"W-w-what d-d-do y-you w-want me t-t-to say?" he stuttered, then coughed, looking very uncomfortable.

"How about, 'Don't beat yourself up about it'?"

"You have t-t-to stop."

"I want to. Get my kid back and split fucking Crack City forever."

"You need help."

"I know I do. I'm gonna go to that Junk-Anon meeting and then work that Ninth Step, make my amends."

"You need psychiatric help."

"No shrinks!" I yelled, and Myron cringed.

"Ed, you scare me." He glugged cough syrup. "Let's pray."

"There's more. There's one more secret —"

"That's enough for today." He gripped my hands hard and we knelt.

"God!" he whispered with feeling. "God, grant me the serenity to accept the things I cannot change, the courage to change the things I can, and the wisdom to know the difference."

"Myron?"

He trembled and coughed, drained the cough syrup, looked at me with scared eyes as I packed my arsenal. "What, Ed?"

"I feel a thousand times better."

THE Junk-Anon meeting, for the loved ones of addicts, in a church basement on Fifty-second Street, already in progress. Women in fur coats, many of them weeping, just a smattering of men. Everyone seemed miserable. Except me. I was joyous as Jumbo the elephant at the end of a five-month bout with constipation. A tall woman with a hawk nose ran the show, recognized the sharers. She pointed at a distraught brunette.

"My name's Leslie, and I'm codependent."

"Hi, Leslie," we chimed; but unlike HDA, there was no enthusiasm.

"Well," Leslie spoke venomously, "he finally did it. My husband got himself arrested for crack possession, and you know something? I'm happy." She laughed hysterically. "Maybe now he'll get off drugs and alcohol and I can get my life back on track. My life!" She rubbed her temples. She was damn good-looking. "I have such a headache. You can't imagine the strain I'm under, trying to find a decent job to pay back our debts." Her voice broke, and she burst into tears. The women on either side put their arms around her shoulders. "I can't take it anymore. I've seen the progression of the disease, and it's awful. He was a beautiful, kind man. Now he's a ninety-eight-pound weasel. Just the other night he came home from a week-long crack and vodka binge and he passed out on the ironing board. I put a quilt on him, and the next morning he was gone, and so was our wedding silver. I'm glad he got busted. I hate him, I hate him, I hate him." Huge tears rolled down her stricken face. "And I love him so much."

"Leslie," twittered Birdbeak. "You can't control it, you didn't cause it, and you can't change it. You must learn to detach from him. Detach with love. Don't be a hostage. Talk with someone after the meeting. Don't stuff those feelings. Let them out. Maybe all this is God's way of saying that you two aren't meant for one another. Maybe it's time to move on."

"My name is Candace, and I'm codependent."

"Hi, Candace," they murmured.

"I'm gay. My lover, Ruth, is a heroin addict, and she dumped me for a man." Candace dissolved into tears. "I loved and nurtured the bitch for five years. I put up with all sorts of shit. How many times did I come home from work — Miss High-and-Mighty never had a job — to find her nodded out in the bathroom, lying in her own vomit? I loved her, and she's dumped me for a breeder! I don't understand!" she wailed.

"Candace. You can't control Ruth. She has her life to live, and you have yours. Maybe it wasn't meant to be. Accept it. Don't stuff the feelings. Use The Program. That's why Farmer Rob's wife, Lilly, founded it. So we could deal with our issues. Maybe it's time to move on, to break the cycle of addiction. Detach with love. You're a worthwhile human being. Don't forget it."

Frank slid in next to me and handed me a steaming cup of coffee.

"Got your message at the hotel," he whispered, petting Natasha.

"This is a great meeting," I said. "Listen to the pain!"

"You're gettin' off on it? Ed, you're a sick fuckin' pup."

"I know. That's why I'm here. To get better. Frank, I need to tell you something." I looked at his eyes and knew I had a friend. "This is my Ninth Step amend to you. I'm sorry I lied last night about my facial scratch."

"And?"

"It's a program of rigorous honesty, so I need to confess." The light of expectation gleamed in his face. "I got into a fight."

Disappointment caked his face like an old hooker's makeup. He wasn't satisfied, but I couldn't tell him; there was something blocking me.

We lit cigarettes, and the women around us glared.

"This is a nonsmoking meeting," one admonished.

"Stuff it, dimples," Frank said nastily. "Focus on yourself."

"No dogs allowed," said a hostile woman in a sable coat.

"She's a codependent," I answered.

"Ed, did you read the *Post?*"

"I've been a little busy, Frank."

"I'm sure you fuckin' have," he said sarcastically, pulling a folded paper from his back pocket. Well, land sakes! Kenny was one busy junkie. Staring from page two was yours truly, head blocked out like in a porno pic, kneeling in rubble, petting Natasha, whose jaws held Too Tall's gold-ringed hand.

"My name is Arthur," announced a dapper black guy in a baggy Armani suit and Vuarnet sunglasses, "and I'm codependent."

"Hi, Arthur."

"Ed, we need to fuckin' talk," said Frank.

"After the meeting," I said. Fear and pride played Ping-Pong with my heart.

"Lord God almighty!" cried Arthur, removing his glasses and rubbing his eyes. "Take this pain away from me. I am a sad and sick son of Baby Jesus and I have nowhere to turn but this blessed Fellowship. I am a victim of this disease. My mama was an alcoholic, my daddy was a drug addict, my granddaddy and his daddy before him were alcoholics. I have lost my wife to this disease, and now I've lost my best employee. What will I do?" His anguished screech sounded like a cat caught in the spokes of a bicycle. Natasha's ears pricked up.

"Arthur." Birdbeak spoke gently. "Disease means dis-ease. Other people's disease causes our dis-ease. It's uncomfortable. Ask for help. Reach out, talk with people after the meeting. If you arrest the disease, the pain does go away. It's not instantaneous; and since we're addicted to addicts, we're just like them, we want everything to be okay immediately. As Lilly said, 'We want what we want and we want it now.' Give time time. There are no quick fixes."

I raised my hand.

"My name is Ed, and I'm a stupid stinking co-dependent."

"Hi, Ed."

"I really identify with Arthur over there. I lost my wife and kids to the disease and I really feel like shit, like a loser. Why me?"

"Ed." Birdbeak had all the answers. "You know what I do when I feel sorry for myself? I fill a baby bottle with apple juice and take a bubble bath. I teethe on the nipple, cry, soak, and then repeat affirmations like 'I am worthwhile and wonderful.' I always feel so much better after; and then when the man arrives with the flowers I sent myself, I can't tell you how happy I am. Try it, you'll like it. You'll feel like a winner."

Frank jabbed me in the ribs. "We gotta talk. Come the fuck outside."

"What is it, Frank?" I asked on the street, in the bright glare of sunshine and fallen snow, already dotted with soot.

He opened the scandal rag.

Snippets about the Hispanic couple, the mushmouth, the bodega dude, Igor and Ivan. My work was getting noticed. It was all over the place. Why, right next to a repeat of yesterday's picture of Too Tall going bye-bye was a close-up of his hand (some neighborhood kids playing in the lot had found it), right above exclusive photos of a bikini-clad Princess Diana. Old Ed was coming up in the world! Next stop, the White House lawn and a Congressional Medal of Honor.

"Aw, she'll do, Frank, but Rachel makes that Limey princess look like a Colonel Sanders reject."

"Hey, asshole, I'm talkin' about that hand, about Natasha's overbite, about drug dealers gettin' offed."

"Drugs are a very dangerous business," I said, feeling pretty fucking proud of the high-profile coverage. "We're lucky to be sober." I couldn't be mad at Kenny. He had the disease. Anyway, it was damned thoughtful of him to block out my face.

"Ed, you can't bullshit a bullshitter."

"Talk English, Frank."

"Fuckit, I'm talkin' 'bout wastin' dealers. I been too busy cheerin' on the home team to really think like a cop; but when the boys called me in this mornin' to get my read, 'cause I'm a fuckin' addict, it clicked. Ed, I feel it in my guts; you're the man. You dusted that Spanish couple, the black guy, those two fat Polacks."

"Ukrainians."

"You even know their fuckin' nationality! That's not in the article. You've been on a fuckin' spree, pal, and I'm warnin' you, you gonna get fucked up the ass."

"Me? I'm worthwhile and wonderful."

"Don't feed me that Junk-Anon crap." Angry-eyed, he lit my cigarette and his own. "Who's that in the picture? Your evil twin? Your dog's evil twin? I'm a cop, numb-nuts, not no dumb fuck. I'm a cop and a junkie, and I know all about resentment and what makes a killer kill."

"Resentment is like pissing all over yourself, Frank. Only you feel it."

"Ed, take that used toilet paper out of your ears and put it in your fuckin' mouth. I know what it's like livin' in your own head. That's a shitty fuckin' neighborhood. I been there."

"Frank, this is a crazy notion you've got. Me a killer?" I laughed.

"Stop dickin' around. You're puttin' me in a sticky fuckin' position. I ain't about to drop a fuckin' dime on you, but it's just a matter of time before they figure it out."

"Figure what out? That I'm detoxing from drugs?"

"Yeah, and it made you fuckin' snap. First that crackerjack Flaco gets nailed and his bull terrier's missin'. Okay, so his is white, yours is black. Both named Natasha? So you paint the dog black and you're off to the fuckin' races. Natasha bites the blimp's hand off, rips the throat off that Doberman in the bodega. How long before Forensics figures the dye-job angle? Natasha's hair is all over the fuckin' place. I shit you not, the boys downtown are close. One fuckin' witness comes forward and you're wearin' a tutu on Rikers Island. Hey fuckface, you listenin'? And that shutterbug who sold the snapshots to the *Post?* You don't think he'll talk? They're lookin' for him right now. The brother you K'd last night? Skin in his brass knuckles." He reached up and slapped my cut face. "Caucasian skin, numb-nuts. Ever heard of DNA testin'? And the broad! What's it feel like to snuff a woman, Ed? I don't know why I'm even talkin' to you. You're a sick motherfucker. I've known some twisted dudes, Ed, and I used to be pretty out there myself, but you, you take the fuckin' cake. How 'bout the shorteyes in the park? That business with the finger, that was real fuckin' cute. How many others? The Polacks? The kid over in Alphabet Land? Shit, you take your act into the real ghetto or any of the projects, numb-nuts, and they'll make Swiss fuckin' cheese out of you and feed you to the rats. In slices. Ed, I'm tellin' you, get the fuck out of Dodge."

"I have been thinking of taking a holiday."

"A holiday? You fantasy-ass dopefiend motherfucker,

you should be shittin' razor blades. Listen to me, bright-boy, I'm stickin' a fork in you: you're done. Take the first fuckin' bus out."

"I appreciate your concern, Frank. I've been asking God to remove my character defects. That's Step Seven, I think. Or is it Six? Anyway, one thing I'm sure of: humility is the way. Once I get my kid back, I'm out of Crack City."

"Ed, I feel for you like a brother. Drop the act. It's pitiful. Get real. Listen to me. No matter how fuckin' much the world loves a vigilante, it's still the cops' job to arrest him. You gotta fuckin' disappear. Otherwise you're dead meat."

"Easy does it, Frank. Don't worry about me. Focus on yourself."

"Ed, baby, you need serious help." The meeting was over and the codependents were glumly filing out.

"You know, Frank, I identify with that guy Arthur."

"You ought to, Ed." He pulled the folded photo of Michelle hanging with the pimps and dealers from his breast pocket. "He's been bangin' the bejesus outta your wife."

"What the fuck you talking about?"

"I saw my buddy in Vice this morning. He put names to these lowlifes. Arthur." He poked a finger at a black guy in the picture. "That's Arthur, douchebag. Arthur Washington. Alias 'Trust.' Trust Washington. Cocaine dealer and player."

The old sickness was upon me.

"Easy fuckin' does it, kool."

Arthur was standing with Leslie, massaging her neck. "Here, Leslie, take one of these." He handed her a fat yellow pill. To the trained eye it looked like a Percodan.

"What is it?" the red-eyed woman asked.

"A chill pill."

She popped it and swallowed.

"Leslie, you're too beautiful to be in such pain." Arthur hugged her. "There are no coincidences in Junk-Anon. God meant us to meet. How would you like to come work for me? I have an opening in my business."

"Is it hard work?"

"No, child, it's simple customer service."

I couldn't take his horseshit, Frank or no Frank. I roped Natasha to a parking meter.

"Wha'sappenin', Jed?" He flashed me a brilliant smile and extended a Rolex-wristed hand. "Thanks for sharing."

I slapped his mitt away, pulled his shades off.

"Hey, man, those are my Vuarnets!" He blinked in the sun.

"Where's Michelle?"

"Who?"

"My wife, asshole," I said, flinging his glasses into the street. "The woman with the two kids."

"Man, you'll pay for those." He shielded his eyes. Leslie gawked.

"Where's my wife?"

"You mean Tiffany? The lady I met here at the Junk-Anon House? I took her in, gave her an excellent position in my firm, and she quit, Jed." He shook his skull and smiled sadly at Leslie, shrugged his padded shoulders. "I'm real sorry about that. She was a good little worker. Some folk are plain ungrateful. I went shopping for new

Reeboks for her boys yesterday, and when I got home they were gone. How's that for gratitude? I don't know if you're aware of this, Jed, but she has a serious problem with drugs."

I got in close to his gloating face and hissed, "So do I, you spineless piece of shit."

Frank jumped in. "Break it up."

"Lady," I said to Leslie, calm as possible, yet trembling. "This guy's a pimp. He'll have you strung out on dope and selling your booty on Eleventh Avenue before the day is out."

"You must be kidding." She laughed. "He's a yuppie."

"Leslie, don't listen to him." The Junk-Anon pimp stroked her shoulders. "The man's crazy with grief. Come with me for cappuccino."

"I'd love to." She smiled goofily. The pill was working already. "How much does the job pay, Arthur?"

He opened the door of a snow-covered BMW, let her in, pulled a parking ticket off the windshield, tore it up, turned and winked at me, then got in the car, rolled down the window and said to the codependent: "Sky's the limit, child, it's piecework sales."

"Thanks for the opportunity, Arthur. You won't be disappointed."

He revved the engine.

"I'm sure I won't. And hey, baby, call me Trust. All the girls do."

WENT home to grab the nineteen thousand and some-
odd dollars I'd earned that week. Soon's I worked the
Ninth Step and got Jeff back, it was adios Crack City.
The other Steps? Hell, it's a lifelong process.

On the staircase, a Popsicle-stick-thin dirt-crusty female with snotty nose dripping down onto a herpes-
scabbed mouth was beaming up.

"Wha'sup, homes? Blow you for five dolla'," she offered, exhaling cracksmoke, scratching her greasy scalp,
starting to scrape the pipe's screen with a pen. "Lick yuh
balls, yuh asshole, evvathang."

"Lips that touch the Devil's Dick shall never touch
mine."

"You ain't down for it, homes, just say no." Her sore-
bumpy lips curled in a sneer and she raised her thin coat
and dirty T-shirt, scratched her bony ribs and potbelly.

"Listen, sis, 'just say no' went out with Nancy
Reagan."

"Loan me five dolla'."

"You pregnant?"

"Yeah, wit' Rosemary's Baby."

"Then hit Rosemary for the five."

"Assho' mafocka!" she screamed at my back.

I cabbed it through the slush up to Eighty-sixth Street. The driver was Romanian and spoke little English. Stopped at the old newsstand I used to terrorize as a kid. Blind John was still there, selling his papers, wore the same dark glasses, only now he had bright white hair and wrinkles.

"Read all about it!" he barked, like newsies of old. "Leonard Lump in Love."

"Hello, John."

"Who's that?"

"You might not remember me. My name's Ed T——, and I grew up around here."

"Eddie T——?"

"The kid who stole all the candy and *Screw* magazines."

"Sure, sure. That dick of yours fall off yet?"

"It's hanging by a thread." Talking ancient history was nice, but I had to work the Ninth Step. "Look, John, I want to apologize and pay you back two C-notes." I peeled the bills. He stroked them and smiled.

"You're a good boy, Eddie. Give my best to your mother."

"I would, John, but she doesn't read *Screw*."

"Hey, Eddie!" he called. "Have a Snickers bar. On the house, for old times' sake."

And when I reached for it, he whacked me with his cane.

"You were a lot faster when you were a kid!"

Driving up through Harlem, drinking strong Spanish coffee (bad for my sobriety to get too tired), eating the Snickers bar (couldn't get too hungry), petting Natasha (shouldn't get too lonely), and trying to control my anger at seeing the post-apocalyptic dirty-snowed cityscape, at the idea of Kenny selling any more photos to the *Post* or telling the cops who I was. The crack and dope trade doing monster biz. Kids hanging on corners, guzzling forty-ounce bottles of malt liquor, making quick exchanges. Five bucks for a five-minute session with Scotty. A quick trip to outer space when they should have been having snowball fights. I was glad to be getting out. Cocaine had wrecked the inner city. It was the national pastime, the Rainbow Plague. It was World War fucking III.

Riverdale. Up on Broadway, the nursing home. Natasha waited in the cab, licking Larry Lamb.

"Look who's here, Mrs. T——," said the nurse changing Ma's diaper.

"Hi, Ma!"

"Who's that?" the old lady croaked. She was thin, wrinkled, balding, liver-spotted. She was watching the afternoon version of "Lifestyles of the Rich and Famous." The nurse handled her like a doll, putting Ma into a bathrobe in seconds flat.

"She's like that sometimes. It's the Alzheimer's. Mrs. T——, it's your son!" the nurse yelled and walked out.

"Who?"

"My name's Ed, and I'm a stu — Ma, it's Eddie."

"Eddie?" She put her oversize round glasses on and peered at me suspiciously. "Eddie? That you? What you doing home from school at this hour?"

"I'm sick, Ma," I said gently. "I have a terminal disease."

"German measles?"

"Yeah, Ma. That's it."

"Sit by me, son. I had the measles when I was young, so it's okay. I'm watching that nice Robert Leach."

I kissed her wrinkled dry cheek. It killed me to see her so far gone.

"Eddie, where's your father?"

"Ma, he's dead."

"That's no way to talk about him. He might drink a little too much, but dead drunk? Nosiree Bob." She shook her head. "You go down to Clancy's and get him. His supper's already cold."

"Ma," I yelled into her ear. "He's here." I picked up the urn of ashes she kept on her bedside table.

"Passed out again?" Ma clucked. "He works so hard." Still the codependent.

"Ma, I'm sorry I was such a rotten kid."

"Stealing from the blind man again? I must have given that poor fellow two hundred dollars for all the stuff you took."

"Forgive me," I said and peeled her three hundreds.

"You got that job at the grocery?"

"No, Ma, I'm a sanitation man, just like Pop."

Ma nodded and with slack toothless jaws watched Robin Leach checking into a luxury château-hotel.

"Pop," I whispered to the urn. "It's good to see you. I'm sorry I hated you. Forgive me. You were sick. You had the disease." I wiped a tear. Finally I was able to mourn him. "I never told you this, Pop, but . . . I love you. You were my hero." I couldn't stop it; I sobbed. "You'd be proud of me. I've got two sons now, and I'm a real patriot. I'm a soldier in the war on drugs." Jesus, I felt a million times better. The Program worked, it truly worked. "Sayonara, Pop."

"Eddie, get your father his supper," she ordered, watching flabby Robin Leach take a Jacuzzi and guzzle champagne with three curvaceous models. "He'll be hungry when he wakes up."

"Ma, I love you." I softly hugged her bony frame.

"Eddie, I know you. When you're nice, you done something bad. What is it this time? You and that Tony La—— been playing with knives again?"

I'D trusted the process, tried to do the right thing, and where had it got me? Facing life behind bars with a lot of penitentiary dicks up my butt to keep me warm nights. Life sucked. Started out sucking Ma's breast, then sucked a milk bottle, on to sucking candy, sucking joints, beers, whiskey, and on and on until I was sucking the Devil's Dick. I'd spent my life sucking on things, and life had ended up sucking. Sucking shit through a sock. Why not follow the old man's example and suck a few bullets from my friendly Glock, the ultimate sucker punch? No, the thing to do was keep working the Steps, give time a little more time, have faith in The Program, trust that Frank was a friend, not a rat.

If Michelle really was trying to start over, to erase the past, to pretend the twelve-year mission of marriage with good old Ed was but a long nightmare, would she not return to the scene of her last self-sufficiency, just another long-legged Midwest yellowhead with stars in her eyes, supporting herself until that big break when she found herself living the dream, prancing upstage at Lincoln Center with Mikey Baryshnikov while the gussied-up likes of Leonard Lump and Sarah Syrup, Count and

Countess Hugo and Baby Luegodago of Uruguay, Larva Shinsplintz, Pepita Lickensplitt, Marmalind and Portius Pleistocene, Evan Bibble-Booth, Muffy Snitbread, Musgrove Messerschmitt, Cleo Klamlapper, the Dreckenzorfer Quintuplets, Fifi, Bibi, Kiki, Lili, and Titi, and all the other perfumed silk-swathed shitheads whose unpronounceable names polluted the gossip columns of the *Post* honored her artistry and grace by politely clapping their diamond-crusted manicured meathooks?

I could smell the Lolita Lounge from half a block away. The sickly sweet 'n' sour stink of stale beer and smoke.

Loud dance music assaulted my ears, jolted my senses. The bar was wall-to-wall scumbags, hanging over drinks, staring and drooling at the wildly gyrating blond up on stage.

Michelle.

I had to turn my head from the familiar nakedness, the wiggling and jiggling flesh I'd sworn to love and honor through sickness and health. My marriage was a three-ring circus, and I was the clown.

Shielding my face in my collar, I made for the pisser, kept on going, knocked and entered the door marked PRIVATE.

A leggy Latino woman whose best days were back in the Nixon administration was pasting tassels on a pair of .44 magnum D cups.

"No customers, man. This is private."

Relief flooded my pre-ulcerous gut. Jeff was snuggled on a couch, sleeping, his bruised face at peace, sucking his thumb, lulled by the music pounding through the walls. Things would be okay.

"No customers allowed back here," said the woman.

I stroked the hair off little Jeff's angelic face. "I'm not a customer," I whispered. "He's my son."

"You don't have to whisper, dude. Tiffany gave the kid two Valiums so's he could sleep."

"That Tiffany's a hell of a mother."

"Hey, man, you know how hard it is finding baby-sitters these days?"

I hoisted Jeff over my shoulder and waded out into the bar.

Michelle's scream cut though "Love Shack" like the guillotine sliced ole Marie Antoinette's aristocratic turkey neck.

"Stop him — he's got my baby!"

I pulled the Glock, freezing the slime where they sat.

"Possession is nine tenths of the law, perverts, and this gun is the balance. Make room for Daddy."

Into the cold sunset glare.

"Ed!" Michelle hugging herself, clad only in G-string and high heels, gold ringlets of hair swept east by vicious Hudson River winds. "He's all I've got," she moaned.

"You still have your figure, Tiffany."

She followed. "Please . . . ," she begged.

"Don't beg; it's disgusting."

"Don't do this." She shivered. "I'll lose my job."

"Out of my face." I made Natasha get on the floor of the cab, laid Jeff gently on the back seat. The Romanian driver sat quietly. He'd seen it all. The meter was up in the hundreds, and I'd already given him a hundred and fifty clams as security.

"You don't want to lose your job, Tiffany."

"My name's Michelle."

A car slowed and stopped, and the driver stared at

my nude wife's breasts bobbing in a sea of frozen gooseflesh.

She screamed, "What's your fucking problem?"

He shook his head and laughed. "Eight million stories in the Naked City, lady; this is just one of them."

I stared at my wife. Desperation in her eyes.

"Michelle, I find this difficult to say." I had to do it, work that Ninth Step, complete the process, make amends, clean up the garbage of my drug life. "I'm truly truly sorry for all the crap I pulled and any pain I caused you and the boys. I was an asshole. Please forgive me."

She bit her lip, hugged her chest, seemed to wrestle with herself, then nodded.

"You coming or what?" I asked.

She jumped in.

"Houston and Bowery." I told the driver.

"You really are an asshole, Ed."

"Yeah, but I'm the asshole you married."

We stared, eyes stabbing blame and pain and hurt, mirror images of misery. Then a strange and wonderful thing happened: the hard years just sort of melted away — it works, it truly works! — her face softened up, and I saw the girl I'd fallen for twelve years back. Sitting beside me in all her naked glory was Michelle Kawalski. We smiled like a pair of twenty-year-old lovebirds facing the future with nothing but hope in our hearts.

She unpinned the wig, plucked it off her head, and chucked it out the window.

"Till death do us part," I said, and kissed the bride.

So they lived happily ever after. . . . And if you buy that you'll also believe that Leonard Lump has renounced all his worldly goods to join the Franciscan monks, is praying eighteen hours a day, subsisting on a diet of coarse bread and water, and flagellating himself whenever an impure thought of Sarah Syrup causes his brown robes to billow into a pup tent.

We put Jeff to bed under the watchful poster eyes of Magic Johnson, called the Kawalskis, told them we'd be out for a visit, spoke to Mutt, who babbled happily about Pa K.'s gun collection — then we retired to the bedroom to consummate the reunion.

"Don't use that thing. I want to feel you inside me."

"Er, umm, don't take this wrong, Michelle, but you have been playing hide-the-salami with total strangers."

"With them I used protection." She touched my hurt face. "And I didn't feel anything; my body was numb with drugs."

"You want to go with me to a meeting later?"

"Why? I'm not an addict. That's the difference between us. I can stop anytime I want. Now that I have my asshole husband back, I don't need to get high. You were a stranger for years, you were disconnected, somewhere else. I watched you fall apart. You were evil."

"I was sick, love, but I'm a whole lot better now."

"You made me feel like a whore in my own bed. It gave me a pain in my heart." She touched her breast.

"I love you. If you only knew the insanity I've gone through since you split. The idea of losing you and the boys made me crazy."

"That's why I turned to the liquor. You were a maniac. It was painful being near you."

"It was painful just being me. I love you, Michelle," I said, stroking her soft thigh, kissing her lips.

"I love you, Ed."

"Can you ever forgive me?"

"I'll consider it," she said, opening her arms. "If you make love to me this instant."

Later — as I nestled between her thighs, flossing my teeth in her silky blondness, feeling intimate and tender and oh-so-in-love, happy like I hadn't been for years, since cutting that deal with Scotty — the doorbell rang. Probably Kenny, here to extort money or dope — or Frank, with his boys. My adrenaline level rocketed. Being nervous was almost like being high. Well, fuckit. Whatever happened, I had to accept it. I jumped into a pair of Jockey shorts.

My heart almost popped from my chest when I saw the cop, a big burly bluecoat, standing there with a tall thin shaved-headed black woman in exquisite clothes.

"Yes?"

"Mr. T——?" asked Mrs. Clean.

"Yes?" I said, scared.

"My name is Prudence DeVore, and —"

"We don't want any."

"I'm from Child Welfare." My fear pulled a Houdini. Everything would be okay.

"You sure you're not from Avon?"

"We're here for the children." She consulted a paper. "Jeffrey and Matthew."

"That's nice of you to offer, but I'm here for them now."

"Sir, I don't believe you're a fit father."

I fell to my hands and gave her twelve push-ups.

"Fit father?" I puffed. "I'm damned fit."

"Very impressive, Mr. T——. But there is the question of child abuse in this case. According to their teacher" — she checked the paper — "Ms. Gonzalez, it seems Jeffrey and Matthew T—— have been exposed to pornography, and there's visual evidence of physical abuse. Both charges constitute automatic grounds for immediate removal from the home. Where are the children?"

"Look, Miss DeVore —"

"Ms."

"Yeah, look, the wife and I have had a rocky time of it lately, but we're back together now and things are fine." I grabbed a pack of Marlboros, lit a cigarette. The welfare woman went into an instant coughing fit. "We've sent Matthew to stay with relatives. Those other things happened when they were with a slime — with their uncle."

"Tell that to the judge. You'll have a fair hearing within forty-eight hours. Until that time we must take custody."

Right then Jeff wandered into the room, rubbing sleep from his eyes, yawning.

"Mommy?" he called.

"Officer," the social worker ordered. "Do your duty."

The cop shrugged. "Sorry, pal," he said, and stepped into the apartment. "C'mere, kid."

"Daddy!" Jeff screamed.

Michelle ran out of the bedroom in a sheer negligee.

"Jeff!" She hugged Jeff's head to her breasts. "Ed, who are these people?"

"They're from Child Welfare. It seems the boys' 'Uncle Arthur' showed them some pornography and hit them."

"Mrs. T——, we're only doing our jobs. You —"

Michelle shrieked and went after Prudence DeVore with both fists. I held her back.

They took Jeff, took him struggling and crying and scared. Michelle wept. I held her close. I was calm. I stuffed my anger. Sometimes it's no good to feel your feelings. I was powerless against the bureaucracy. Had to accept life on life's terms. I was getting used to shit going haywire. Had to let go and let God.

"Michelle, we'll get him back. We just have to stay straight and trust the process. We'll see the judge in two days, and then it's hasta luego Crack City. Just be patient. All right?"

"I'd like to shoot that bitch."

"Violence isn't the answer."

"Then what's the gun for, Ed? Show-and-tell?"

"For the hell of it, darling."

There was a faraway look in her eyes as she wandered into the bedroom.

"Michelle, you okay?"

"Nothing a little drink won't cure."

THE Program works if you work it, I knew, and after racking my brains as to where I'd fucked up, I realized that my Ninth Step was incomplete. There was one major amend I had yet to make.

I let my fingers do the walking for an address. Michelle stood there staring out the window onto the Bowery. She swore she wouldn't get buzzed. Not that I really believed her, but what was I going to do — spend the rest of my life keeping things out of her mouth? So I left her hanging with Natasha. I had to work The Program.

I took a three-cigarette cab ride uptown to a fancy Park Avenue building.

The impeccably uniformed doorman cast snooty eyes on my ratty longcoat, grubby jeans, and beat sneakers.

"Deliveries in the back," he sneered from beneath his oversized military hat.

"I'm here to see Hunter Lodge, Jr.," I announced.

"Your name?" he asked, with obvious distaste.

"The Leech."

"Mr. Lodge?" He spoke into the house phone. "Mr. Leach here to see you." He looked at me as if I were a particularly unpleasant bowel movement, listened for a moment, shrugged his gold-epauleted shoulders. "No, sir. . . . Yes, sir. Very well, sir."

"He thinks you're Robin Leach," he informed me haughtily. "Eleventh floor."

"Which apartment, Admiral Poindexter?"

"There is only one apartment."

I rode the wood-paneled car up to eleven, exited into a marble-floored foyer, and knocked on the door.

"It's open," called a chillingly familiar voice. "Come on in, Robin."

A fucking palace. Chandeliers, Picassos, Van Goghs, Persian rugs, weird sculptures, shiny antiques, and there, lying on a couch in front of a big-screen TV, watching "Jeopardy," was the guy I'd hated all these years, the richboy scumbag who'd caused me such pain, fucked my life silly.

No, I thought, no. I'd made my life a mess. I'd resented this putz for ages, and it had been like pissing all over myself. The only one who'd felt it was me. And it had made me stink, made my thinking stink. Now I was cleaning up, wiping the slate with an apology, and God would reward me by returning my son and issuing our little family a ticket to ride.

A half-eaten pizza on the table, next to an empty bottle of Jack Daniel's and one half full.

"Bring the cameras in," said Hunter Lodge, Jr., handsome still, blond still, unchanged from near twenty years ago. He wore a pink alligator shirt, beige corduroy pants, and brown penny loafers without socks. His Rolexed hand went for the Jack Daniel's.

"Wrong leech," I said, standing under a chandelier,

feeling the weight of my weapons in my pocket. "I'm not Robin." He looked at me for the first time.

"No, you're not. Why are you here? Deliveries in the back." He guzzled from the bottle.

"I'm here to get something off my chest. You might not remember me."

"I certainly do not." His nostrils flared as he scrutinized me head to toe.

"You knew me at St. Dismas. I was the Leech."

"The Leech?" He scratched his ass. "I don't remember. . . . Wait, are you the guy . . . the guy we, umm, the guy who stole all that shit and we had to . . ."

"Nutty."

"Correct. The guy we nuttied."

"You nuttied."

"How are you, guy? Long time no see. What a surprise! Sit down." He smiled, showing a mouthful of exquisite teeth. "Please, make yourself comfortable."

I sat.

"What's up . . . ? I forgot your name."

"I thought a Lodge never forgets."

"Yes, well . . ."

"Ed."

"Qué pasa, Ned? You want a drink?" I shook no. "A beer?" He scooted over to a bar fridge. "Heineken, Beck's, Amstel Light, Coors, Corona, Anchor Steam, Dos Equis, Grolsch?"

"Grolsch?" My scrotum tightened.

He brought me a green-bottled Grolsch and a glass. "I don't drink," I said through gritted teeth.

"That right?" He smiled. "You don't mind if I do?" He opened the Grolsch, poured, and guzzled.

"Well, Ned, qué pasa, dude? I occasionally wondered how you were. I felt somewhat bad about that nutty incident. My psychiatrist attributed the whole thing to latent homosexuality, said I had a castration complex or some such malarkey. He blamed it on Mumsy."

"Why? Mumsy didn't nutty me. Did Mumsy nutty you?" But that wasn't what I was there for; that wasn't the Ninth Step. "Look, Hunter, I need to apologize. I've been harboring a resentment for many years. Please forgive me."

"Don't be silly." He giggled and reached onto the black marble coffee table, opened a silver Tiffany box full of sparkling white powder. "Have a line. Let's seal this business forever."

My legs went weak, my armpits sweaty.

Hunter Lodge, Jr., spooned a gram or two onto the black table, chopped with a platinum American Express credit card, expertly spread lines, and then snorfled. He passed me the silver straw.

I stared at the coke. It was radiant.

He flipped channels on the tube and sniffed.

"How do you like the place, Ned?"

"Ed." I laid the straw down. God, it looked delicious.

"Ed. My folks died and left it to me."

"My condolences."

"Don't be silly. It was their time, and I'm lucky they expired, God rest their selfish souls." He rubbed his nose. "I was working for Drexel when the market crashed. The company went belly-up, and I was out of a job. My fiancée dumped me, and I started seeing the shrink. A little crisis demonstrates who really cares about you. The parental unit couldn't have kicked the bucket at a more opportune moment." He sniffled and rubbed his nose. "Have some schnitz. It's outrageous."

"No thanks." I got up to go. "I said what I needed to."

"Don't go, Ned." He guzzled Grolsch. Fancy that! Hunter Lodge, Jr., was lonely. Lonely at the bottom, lonely at the top. "Let's watch the cable news." He pulled me down, ate a pill chased with beer. "I'm taking this Prozac shit, medication for depression. You look somewhat bummed. Care for some?"

"Not today. Have you thought about quitting coke?"

"Are you serious? Blow is good for me. I don't know what I'd do without it. It's made me realize I don't need anybody. I fired my butler, my valet." He tooted another line. The disease had him. From park benches to Park Avenue, it wanted all of us dead. "My maid comes in the mornings and leaves by the time I get up. I don't have to see anyone I don't want to. It's paradise. I have unlimited cocaine, television, two hundred and sixty million dollars, and one of the finest private art collections in the world. Who could ask for anything more? Okay, hookers now and then, and my barber, and the shrink five days a week; but for me they all make house calls. Occasionally a friend stops over for a few ounces, and I'll sell it to them, for just a slight profit, just to keep sharp, but they're not friends, they're assholes." He smiled at me. "It's nice to have a real visitor. A blast from the past." He nose-vacuumed another line and sighed. "Check this shit out."

The cable news was doing a heart-wrenching piece on child leprosy in Africa. A deep sadness overwhelmed me. Poor children, scrawny, missing legs, arms, noses, fingers, flesh rotting and covered with flies and festering sores, rejected by other children, pelted with stones and stares and curses, cast out of their hometowns, ignored by the world, isolated in compounds. Their tortured eyes were pools of misery, the despair of a cruel universe was reflected in their innocent faces. And they'd accepted it, the fight had been beaten out of them. Their disease was progressive, incurable, and they knew it. Maybe with research . . .

"Don't tell me you buy this bleeding-heart bullshit?" Lodge snorted a line.

"That's the real deal, man," I said, feeling tears.

"Well, at least it's not us. Have a line."

"Hunter." I looked at his stupid coked face and grinding jaw. "What if you died suddenly? Who gets your money?"

"My shrink, of course."

"Do me a favor," I said. "I know this sounds strange, but as a joke, make a new will and leave the dough to these children."

"Why ever would I do that? They don't do a goddamn thing for me."

Powerless? Hell no. God? What kind of God would afflict these poor beautiful souls and let them live a life of rot and rejection. What kind of God would allow babies to be born with AIDS or come into this sad broken world all addicted to crack, twisted in body and jonesing for coke from the get-go? What kind of God —

"Think of it as a way of finding out if your shrink cares for you or for your money."

"Superlative thinking, Ned." He guzzled from the Jack Daniel's, got up and went to a desk, pulled a piece of monogrammed paper, and wrote with a gold fountain pen. "You know, Ned, these worthless jungle bunnies deserve what they get." He spoke matter-of-factly, as if we were partners in some stock market scam. "They're not white, like us. They're less than human. I mean, I have a social conscience, but really we are the superior race and —"

"Sign it."

He affixed his signature, blew on the paper to dry the ink, then took a sip of whiskey and cleared his throat. " 'I, Hunter Lodge, Jr.,' " he read, " 'being of sound mind and body, do hereby bequeath all my holdings to the little lepers of the Third World.' " He laughed. "How's that?"

"That's fine. Date it last year."

"Okay." He dated the document, tucked it in his desk drawer. "My shrink will really get a kick out of this." He giggled. "Now how about a healthy drink and a line?"

He went and grabbed a fresh Grolsch, poured a glass, took a long drink, sat at the table, and spread a line.

"And I thought you were Robin Leach!" He chortled.

More like Robin Hood.

"So, old sport, how about some polo on Saturday?"

"Goodbye, Hunter."

"Tennis? Croquet? Come with me to Nantucket."

"Say your prayers, pal." I put the silenced Glock against his blond head. "It's bedtime."

"What's that?"

"It's the King Ed version of the Bible, Jack."

"Stop joking — have a line. That business about the will —"

"Turn our will and our life over to the care of . . . to

215

the care of Ed. Sorry, richboy, you've come to the end of the lines."

"What? I'm meeting Grandmumsy at Au Bar later. You want a Picasso? Tickets to *Les Misérables?* Cash? In the desk drawer."

"This won't hurt a bit," I said.

"Why, Ed? Why?"

"A man's gotta believe in something, Hunter," I explained, though I'm sure he didn't understand. His type never does. The Leonard Lumps, the Papa Docs, the Pol Pots — they take and take and steamroll lives without ever considering their victims. "An eye for an eye just sort of feels right."

An ungentlemanly aroma wafted from his pants. His face fell apart and his upper lip did a jitterbug. He leaned over and snorted more coke. Got on his knees.

"For the love of Christ, Ed, don't do this."

"Grolsch, Junior, this is for the children," I said, and blasted away at his worthless blond head, blowing his handsome face all over the TV screen.

As I stuffed the lining of my coat with packs of five-hundred-dollar bills, I had to laugh. Rich, poor, black, white, an asshole is an asshole. They all died the same. I took a last look at Hunter Lodge, Jr. A chunk of his patrician nose was floating in the half-drunk glass of Grolsch, staining the beer a pretty raspberry color. It almost matched his alligator shirt. "What the hell," I said aloud. "Tradition calls for a nutty." So I shot him in the testicles and hummed the St. Dismas fight song.

"I'm here to see Rachel."

A couple of depressed-looking tits drooped through a black fishnet bra and jiggled as she barked, "On your knees, slave, and service your mistress." She cracked a riding crop across her desk. "Welcome to Whips R Us," she added pleasantly, shaking her chickenfeather mop and glaring from overly mascaraed eyes. "Do you have an appointment to see Mistress Rachel?"

I shook no.

"Aren't you ashamed?"

"No."

"Suck and fuck and cook and clean. That's your pre-scribed routine."

"Tell her it's Ed and I left my apron at home." I whiffed deep on the circus of smells — cheap perfume, new leather, old sweat, and disinfectant — listened to a Valentine's Day sampler of muffled squeals, grunts, and groans from the rooms off the reception area.

She appraised my body, punched an intercom, and spoke into a desk phone. "Mistress Rachel, there's a vile revolting putrid undisciplined piece of garbage named

Ed to see you." And then to me: "Second door to your left, slime."

Rachel stood there decked out in mistress fatigues: black leather window bra, fishnet stockings, garters snapped onto peekaboo panties, whip in hand. She looked ravishing.

"Oh, Ed!" she cried, just a sweet girl under all those layers of dark. And then she was in my arms. "I was having the worst anxiety attack. I —"

"Inhale faith, exhale fear. That's what Myron says." I stroked her baby's-behind soft black hair, kissing her neck, rubbing her collarbone with my lips.

"Don't quote that old queen to me." She was annoyed.

"Rachel, Myron is saving my life on a daily basis."

"Then let him suck your cock."

"Rachel, what's with you?"

"I just have this terrible feeling," she said, shivering.

"Feelings aren't facts."

"Fuck the slogans. Why are you here, Ed?"

"I did my Fifth Step," I said, circling around the reason for my visit.

"That's nice," she said, dull as a mental patient after a megadose of Thorazine.

"And I did the Sixth, Seventh, Eighth, and Ninth, I think, and —"

"That's nice," she muttered without feeling.

"And I saw my mother," I said, patting her muscled rump. Circling, still circling. "And I made an amend to her and to my father, who's dead." I licked a stiff nipple. "And to this old blind guy I used to steal from and —" Circling and circling, like Natasha before taking a dump.

Circling. Prancing in a maddening dance. Out with it, Ed. "And I got my wife back."

"There it is," she whispered. I stepped back and looked at her. A single mascara-black tear snaked down her cheek and dripped onto her leather bra.

"But baby," I said, kneeling, burying my head in her black pubic hair, "I love you. That hasn't changed. We'll go away somewhere. Just you and me and Michelle and the boys. It's God's will."

At that her shoulders started heaving.

"Don't cry, little one."

"Cry?" she shrieked. "You idiot. I'm laughing. What kind of asshole do you take me for?"

She pushed my head away, and I stared at her steel-toed cowboy boot. She was laughing at me.

"Come on, Rachel."

"Lick my boots, slave."

"Cut the shit, Rachel."

She stepped back, flicked her whip, and nailed me on the shoulder.

"Ouch," I said. "You hurt me."

"I hurt you? Motherfucker." She spoke bitterly. "That'll teach you. I'm not some kind of plaything. I'm not a Barbie Doll or a whore you can just manipulate. I have feelings."

"I love you, Rachel. That hasn't changed."

"Yeah right. And we'll live like Mormons in Utah. Just you, me, the crackhead kids, and the happy hooker. I love you too, Ed. You're mine. It's a selfish program, and I have no intention of sharing," she said nastily, picking up a foot-long dildo that buzzed and vibrated.

"Pull your pants down, bitch, and I'll take your temperature."

I got up and moved away from the plastic penis. I really really didn't want to lose her. She was sweet, she was gorgeous, she was a hundred-and-ninety-eight-proof thoroughbred nymphomaniac. What more could a man want? But hey, this was a side of her I'd never seen before.

"Uh, Rachel," I said, backing toward the door, reaching into my pocket. "How would you like tickets to *Les Misérables?*"

ONE less girlfriend, but a grand total of a hundred and sixteen thousand plus dollars and a Rolex! Downtown in a cab, the longcoat lining stuffed with bills. I felt happy, joyous and free; all my doubts had washed away. It was a selfish program, and it worked, it truly worked!

Myron buzzed me in.

He was still wearing the same robe and slippers.

"Zh-zh-zh!" he mumbled, face all a mess, lipstick smeared on his chin, mascara running from puffy eyes. "Murdurra."

"Myron, are you sick?"

His glassy pained eyes judged me with contempt. He slumped on the couch and laughed. He stunk like twelve winos in a phone booth. " 'M only as sick as your secrets." He laughed some more.

"Myron, you're drunk."

"No shit, Egg. M'name's Myron, not Moron. Drunky drunk. Feels great, scumbag. Love it. Fanks."

"Thanks?"

"You meh me do it, killah."

"I don't have that kind of power."

"Your Fiff Step made me step ou' fo' a fiff." He giggled

221

and drained a bottle of Stolichnaya. "Couldn't afford this fancy shit in ol' days. Love it. 'S Big Jim said, 'Once a pickle, never a cucumber.' Or was it Farmer Rob?"

"Myron," I said, lighting a smoke, looking around the trashed apartment. "I didn't cause it. You chose it. You drank because you're an alcoholic. Simple as that."

Big fat tears rolled down his wrinkled cheeks.

"Stop that, Myron. You're a big boy now."

"Not a boy, Eggie, 'm a woman," he said sobbing. " 'M gonna get fired from my job an' then I'll never get my operation." He whined, " 'S your fault. All those years downa drain."

"Don't beat yourself up about it."

"Slogans slogans slogans. 'M sick of slogans."

"Myron, I'm working my Ninth Step and I want to make it up to you."

"Fin' 'nother sponsor. You're fired, you piece o' shit." He jumped up, searching. "Shit, I need a drink." He reeled over to the bathroom, came out with —

"Myron, don't!"

He guzzled the Obsession perfume, threw the empty over his shoulder. "Ahh!" He patted his belly. "Tha' hits the spot."

I walked him around, tried to sober him up.

"Hey, sailor." He pinched my butt. "Lez dance."

"How about a meeting?"

"Fuck tha' shit. 'M gonna enjoy my drunk. Put some Streisand on the hi-fi."

"What are you, a masochist?"

Somehow I poured Myron into a pair of jeans, a T-shirt, and a leather jacket, washed his face, put on his cowboy boots, stuffed a suitcase, guided him out into the air, hailed a cab.

"Where we going, Egg," he asked, applying makeup. "T' detox?"

"You'll see."

"Egg, 'm sorry I got drunk." He burped a perfume burp, and the car smelled all pretty and seductive.

"Don't beat yourself up about it."

Out in Queens, I had the driver pull off the highway and stop at a gas station so I could buy a pack of smokes. I turned from the glass booth. Myron had his lips wrapped around a gas nozzle, sucking hard.

"Myron!" I ran, pulled the pump from his mouth. Gas dribbled onto his chin. Lipstick stained the metal.

"Yummy." He sighed, holding on to the pump, licking his lips. "Super unleaded.

"Let go and let God, Myron."

As we drove, Myron had his head out the window, puking his guts out, crying.

"I hate myself, Ed. I hate myself," he said, sobbing. "I'm so lonely, so stupid, so worthless."

I smoothed his hair. "This too shall pass."

"Y'know what?" my sponsor asked, sweating.

"What?"

"The Program ruins drinking." His voice sober from throwing up, the cab smelling of perfume and gas from his perspiration. "It's no fun anymore." He sighed. "As Big Jim said, 'A belly full of liquor and a belly full of HDA just don't mix.' "

We rode along in silence, the Van Wyck Expressway roadside snow crusted black from exhaust fumes.

"Kennedy Airport? Where we going?"

"Not 'we,' babydoll; you."

"Ed?" He belched gas. "I don't want to go to rehab."

"Trust me," I said, paying the taxi.

"Yeah?"

"And promise me you won't ever drink again."

"No one can promise that." We entered the TWA terminal. I toted the suitcase. "But I won't drink today. Just for today. I'm starting a fresh twenty-four hours right now."

"Good boy."

"Girl."

"Sorry. Good girl. Now you sit over in that coffee shop and drink some hot java while I see to things."

Ten minutes later, I had the ticket and an issue of *Vogue*.

"Here." I gave them to him. "We have to hurry." We walked, arm in arm, through the airport bustle.

"Is this a good rehab I'm going to?"

"The best."

"Why are you doing this?" he asked, opening the ticket.

"Because I love you, and I'm grateful for all you've done for me. And to stay sober I need to help another sick and suffering addict. The Twelfth Step. You taught me that."

"What's this, first class to London?"

"Forty-minute stopover, and you change planes. Then it's on to Copenhagen."

"Denmark?"

"Isn't that where the best sex-change doctors are?"

"I don't have that kind of money."

I stopped, unlatched the suitcase, showed him an even hundred grand cash nestled among his training bras, panties, passport, and portraits of Big Jim and Farmer Rob. "You do now."

"Ed, I love you." He fixed me with joyous black eyes, started to cry. "I don't know what to say."

"How about, 'Don't beat yourself up about it'?" I said, and we both laughed.

"But Ed," he said, worried. "Can you afford it?"

"It's only money, Myron. I worked hard for it, and I want you to have it. I insist."

"Ticket, please," said the woman at the metal detector. "Better hurry."

"Ed, how can I ever repay you?"

"Don't drink, and go to meetings, and don't buy any Exxon stock."

"Can you forgive me those terrible things I called you?"

"Sticks and stones. . . . What you said is the truth, Myron, and HDA is a program of rigorous honesty. I have to accept reality." I hugged his warm sobbing body, felt his girlish breasts trembling. Then he turned, strode through the security arches, head held proud and high. A real fighter.

"Bon voyage!" I called.

He wheeled and waved; and only then did I realize I, too, was crying. "Bon voyage," I whispered. "Bon voyage, Myra."

MY wife was not at home. Just Natasha and a note. "A Frank called — needs to talk. That creep Kenny called, said to tell you he was sorry — needs cash for some pictures? Some bimbo named Rachel phoned. Said she got soap opera part. Said you were a good fuck. Called me names. How could you?"

Natasha sat quiet and still at my side on the cab seat. I had the driver cruise by the Convention Center stroll. No Michelle, just a group of hookers, including Leslie from the Junk-Anon meeting, turned out in high heels and spandex.

My insides boiled. Fuckit, I'd slept with one woman; and I'd loved Rachel, really loved her. How many men had Michelle blown or banged? Pornographic images flooded my headspace. The disease had taken her prisoner. That stupid stinking disease! It was the enemy. It wanted to mock me, debilitate me, make me feel like a worthless chump — one day at a time it wanted me dead.

Dropped by the HDA Center on the anorexic chance Michelle had conquered her denial and was getting some help. Under the bright fluorescent light, which illuminated pimples and greasy foreheads, brown-bagged eyes and soup-stained shirts, I scanned for my mate. She wasn't there. Over in the corner, Frank and Rachel were whispering to each other. Good, they belonged together. Where was Michelle?

"Thirty-fifth Street," I told the cabbie. "And make it sudden."

He tore up Third Avenue. I jammed a fresh clip into the Glock.

"Keep the change."

I kicked the glass of the entrance door, reached inside, and turned the handle. We silently climbed the plush stairs.

Trust the process? I'd process the Trust.

"Quiet, Natasha." She was bristling, growling low. Through the door I heard the voice I'd grown to hate, that nauseating Robin Leach, singing the praises of the good life, selling the impossible dream to a nation drunk on fantasy and consumption, a nation that numbly dumbly worshiped celebrities and ignored the needs of starving children while pounding back the Budweiser, a nation that elected a President who wanted to fight the war on drugs with an army of caterpillars.

I pulled the dog aside, shot the lock off the door. Life on life's terms?

They didn't even notice me.

In the flickering glare of the TV, Arthur "Trust" Washington, naked save for a Rolex, was pumping my wife on the couch.

"Show's over." I shoved the Glock in his ear.

The Junk-Anon pimp disengaged, laughed, rose, put his hands high, walked backward to the wall.

Michelle was passed out, colored blue in the light of the tube, and bleeding from her sex. I could see the spike holes in her arm.

Robin Leach yammered about duck hunting in Scotland.

"Shit, Jed, you ain't got the balls to use that toy." He smirked. "Tiffany come back to Trust 'cause you just can't get the job done with that gherkin pickle you call a johnson." He swung his condom-covered wilting wiener. "You don't got one of these."

"You fucking skank, she came to you for drugs," I said, feeling the cold sickness washing over me as I looked at Michelle lying there comatose, blood pooling between her thighs. "You want to play kiddie games?" I smiled. "I have something you don't."

"What's that, homeboy?"

"The disease," I said, firing the Glock, plugging him in both shoulders, one thigh, one wrist. "Die slow, pimp motherfucker."

He screamed, slid down the wall, making funny barnyard noises.

"Sweetheart, naptime's over," I said, kissing Michelle's chilled lips, watching the Junk-Anon pimp bleed, hearing him yelp and moan as Robin Leach, wearing a kilt, sipped ale in a Scottish pub.

"Get up!" I yelled in her face.

Nada.

A used syringe, two torn and empty bags of dope, a

charred spoon, a book of matches, and a belt. In the flickering light of the tube, I could see she really was blue, bright blue, and still bleeding.

"Get up, you crazy bitch!" I slapped her cheeks.

"She wanted it, Jed," Trust rattled between moans, groans, and grunts. "She wanted the dope."

"Did she?" I sighted the Glock at his forehead.

"Yo, man. Ain't my fault she's a junkie. Call 911."

"Let me get this straight." I lowered the gun. "It's not your fault she's a junkie crackerjack whore'?"

"We were having Chinese food."

"And the fortune cookie suggested a casual rape after you fixed her with a hot shot?"

"I used a condom."

"Aren't you considerate," I said, going over and punting his kisser. "Sorry it's not a Pump."

"You want drugs?" he whimpered from his bloody mouth. "Big piece of rock in the closet. It's yours," he rasped. "Just don't lemme bleed to death."

"That's precisely what I intend to do."

I let go Natasha's rope, picked Michelle up, and walked her limp body around the room.

Natasha dropped the lamb and started to lick Trust's bleeding thigh. Trust moaned and feebly tried to push her away.

Robin Leach was now in England, visiting the crown jewels with — I had to laugh — with stunning starlet Sarah Syrup.

I laid Michelle on the floor, put my lips to hers and blew air, paused, thumped her chest, blew again. "Come on, honey, live," I whispered, and repeated the process.

Trust let loose a scream that drowned out Robin Leach.

"Natasha!" I called.

She turned to me and, in her grinning sharkjaws: Trust's pecker.

"Detach with love," I said, laughing and laughing as Trust screamed and screamed, grabbed his bleeding crotch. Natasha shook her head, flinging pimp blood all over the place.

"Let's get out of here," I said. Michelle was making little moaning sounds. I slapped her cheeks, put her jeans and shirt and sneakers on.

"C'mon, Natasha, let go."

"Please, call the paramedics," groaned Trust, holding his wounded groin.

"Drop it, Natasha."

She shook her head side to side.

I grabbed Larry Lamb and waved it. Her jaws relaxed, and the dingus hit the carpet. Natasha picked her little pal up.

"Put it on ice, Jed," sputtered the pimp.

"Good idea, Arthur." I went to the kitchen, filled a large pot with ice and water, grabbed a pair of chopsticks from a half-eaten carton of moo goo gai pan. I immersed Michelle's hands up to the wrists in the cold pot. She was breathing steadily now.

I plucked Trust's dong up with chopsticks. "That's one blow job you won't forget," I said, walking.

And before I flushed, I spat.

I carried Michelle out, Natasha and Larry Lamb at my knee. Looking back, I saw the pimp crawling for the phone. Robin Leach was being received by the Queen of England.

"How 'bout them apples?" I asked my beloved, as her dope-heavy eyelids lifted. "Robin's hit the big time."

Michelle moaned. Her blue eyes focused on me, and in a strangled voice heavy with mucus and heroin, she muttered, "Beam me up, Scotty."

I SAT there in the dark for a long time, staring at Michelle sleeping peacefully, dope-snoring. My wife. I loved her. I stroked her hair, sang a lullaby, listened to the ticking clock, glanced at my two Rolexes, smoked a cigarette. It tasted like shit. I stubbed it out. Time to quit smoking. Just another drug to keep the underclass enslaved and dying slow. In a couple of hours we'd go to a hotel. God, I was tired. Enough was enough. My eyes ached.

"Just you and me, Natasha," I said and stroked the smiling dog. Her breath on my hand was warm. "It's a program of rigorous honesty, baby, and there's something I need to share." She licked my cold fingers. "My old man had cancer. He was on his way out. It's a hot summer night, and I come home from an LSD, beer, and reefer party. Here I am, floating — young, in good health . . . I mean, I'm juiced up with life, and I get home and there's Pop in his chair, looking old and sad and wasted. A sorry in-pain motherfucker sucking on a whiskey bottle. Ma's asleep. Pop's got this pearl-handled revolver. And dig this, Natasha: he's crying. That big tough cock-diesel motherfucker was weeping. A first." Natasha eyed me curiously, her ears perking at the tone of wonder in my voice. "He's crying, and he says, 'Son, I love you.' Another first. He'd never ever said that. Never. So he passes me the whiskey and tells me to have a shot. And I do. It goes down like water, and then he takes one, and he says, 'I gave you life, Ed, and you gotta help me.' Now I'm crying too." And sitting there in the dark with the dog, Michelle's snores steady as shore-washing waves, I felt wet salt tears on my lips. "He hands me the gun, Natasha. Again, he tells me he loves me and says, 'Do it, Ed. Help me, son.' And it's like I'm in a trance. I see myself lift the gun. I stick it in his mouth. He's holding my hand and smiling with his eyes, and, Natasha, I did it, I pulled the trigger."

There, I'd said it. My secret. My only remaining secret. The one I'd never shared with anybody.

"And, girl, at the moment I shot him, as I watched his brains and blood soak his favorite chair, watched his face cave in, his body relax, girl, I loved him so much, like I'd never loved him before. I put the gun in his hand and hugged him. And then Ma was there, crying. And that was it. I shot heroin for the funeral. That's it." I wiped my nose, listened to the ticking clock, my snoring wife, to traffic vrooming, horns bleating, and sirens wailing, watched car lights race across the ceiling. I took Natasha onto my lap, and she lay there, hot and dark and heavy. I sat there for a long time. I had finally told someone. I was at peace with myself. Hell, I was cured.

The phone rang, insistent. I picked it up, listened.

"Ed?" It was Rachel. She sounded scared. "Ed, are you there?" Her voice was agitated. Natasha groaned in her sleep.

"Yeah," I said. "What is it now?"

233

"Please," she whispered, desperate. "I have a problem."

"So do I, girlfriend. I'm a stupid stinking drug addict and alcoholic."

"Ed, Shorty's here. In the kitchen. He's got the enema bag and he's filling it with Perrier and cocaine. He already raped me and now he wants me to — Come quick!" The line went dead.

Jesus, I thought, putting Natasha down, lacing my sneakers, putting my coat on, when will it end? The Program works if you work it, so I had to go, had to help another sick and suffering addict, even if she'd almost wrecked my marriage and nearly gotten my wife killed with her jealous phone call. I kissed Michelle lightly on the lips, petted the pooch, then headed out, once again, into the cold.

A two-minute cab ride dropped me at Rachel's place. I still had her keys. Let myself in the front door, ran up the stairs, listened at her apartment. All was quiet. I stuck the key in the door, turned the lock, entered.

There was Rachel, naked, upside down, hanging from inversion boots, sobbing, tears running down her forehead, dripping onto the floor, her hair spreading groundward like a great plume of black peacock feathers, a tube emerging from her rear, an enema bag lying on the floor next to an almost empty Perrier bottle and a foil packet of white powder. And in the chair — I couldn't see his body, his back was to me, only a mass of long black hair — there in the chair, the famous Shorty.

"Don't, Shorty, don't," she whined. "I don't want to get high."

I pulled the Glock, aimed it at the black hair.

"Don't worry, Rachel," I said, bone-tired, hatred for Shorty stoking me. "Every little thing's gonna be all right." And I pressed the trigger, blew the motherfucker's head apart. Black hair and chunks of skull flew. It looked like a goddamn watermelon, all red, split, and dripping. I laughed at the image. "Fucking slimebucket dealer," I said, putting my gun away. "It's over, Rachel."

I sure was gonna miss the killing, the blood, the adventure, that sweet adrenaline high. Hell, I'd finally found something better than drugs, something I was good at, something I was really good at. They couldn't take that away.

Prison.

Turns out it was a watermelon. A watermelon and a wig.

"Why, Rachel? Why?" I asked, feeling the cold metal bracelets, the room crawling with cops, including Frank.

"It's a selfish program, Ed," she said, naked, unembarrassed, voice cold as a financier's heart. As an officer read me my rights, she pulled on a pair of lacy black panties, took a guzzle of Perrier, wiped her wet forehead; and that's how I'll remember her for always, till the meat of time flakes off the bones of the universe.

"Frank, you skunk, you betrayed me."

"Hey, babe, it's the American way. Don't fuckin' beat yourself up about it. It's called arrestin' the disease."

"I thought we were friends."

"Friends is one thing, numb-nuts, but business is business. You were gonna get popped anyway. I'll visit you upstate."

"Hey!" he blurted. "That's my old Glock!"

"It's evidence now," said a cop.

Just goes to show, there are no coincidences in HDA. Rachel was spooning Oreo Crunch ice cream from the carton into her pretty little yap. I got down on my knees and — remembering what Big Jim had said about never getting too hungry, angry, lonely, or tired — picked up a hunk of watermelon. I ate it with gusto, the sweet water running down my chin. And as they led me out, and down the steps, I spat seeds and laughed.

The joint is all about living life on life's terms, one day at a time. I've quit smoking cigarettes, and Monday through Friday I watch Rachel on the soap opera. I had to forgive her. It turns out I made her pregnant. Our baby was the first ever born live on a daytime soap. It was exciting. I passed out cigars, and the prison population cheered.

I got Michelle pregnant too. I guess those first days in The Program I wasn't shooting blanks. They both came to court in the family way. The *Post* had a field day, dubbed me "The Village Vigilante," "mean and sober Ed T———," "The Glock Gunner." I graced the cover of the paper countless times — hell, more than Leonard Lump ever did. Sure, I confessed. What else could I do? It's a program of rigorous honesty.

Natasha had shed her black hair and was shimmering her natural white. Myra was back from Denmark, a total woman, stunning, glowing. She'd even had enough money for breast implants. Rachel was gorgeous. Michelle was beyond beautiful. Kenny had found The Program, was clean and happy, and his book, with a picture of me and Natasha on the cover, was number one with a bullet. The kids were there too, off drugs. Everyone was sober, even witnesses like Clarence (Wonder Bread) and Leslie from the Junk-Anon meeting. And Ed? Ed was just Ed, a humble veteran of the war on drugs. The citizens of Crack City ate it up. I'm still answering all your supportive letters and cards.

I'm divorced now. I can't blame Michelle. Why stay married to a guy serving multiple twenty-five-year-to-life sentences? I'm here for ever, one day at a time, for fucking ever. My ex-wife and Frank are getting hitched in the fall. He's been a big help to her, and he's back on the force, much decorated. Frank's a good father to Donatello and Jeff. The skunk also plans on adopting Baby Ed once he and Michelle get married. The kids are both in therapy and daily attend Junk-Ateen meetings. Natasha lives with the family, and they tell me she's an excellent companion; but hey, I already knew that.

Time passes. Everyone is clean and serene. Funny how their lives got better once old Ed was out of circulation. Even Kenny. He's still sober. *Crack City* won the Pulitzer, and he's rich. I see him on Oprah and Letterman and Arsenio Hall, and his picture is in the *Post* all the time, in the company of one gorgeous model or rich girl after another. For a while there was a rumor he was set to marry Muffy Snitbread, the laxative heiress. I'm proud of him. It's like I was a walking talking disease, infecting everyone with my sickness. I waxed eleven people (I count Natasha's kill, and so did the law), and the twelfth, well, I figure I was the twelfth. I'm a new man; and I owe it all to Hard Drugs Anonymous.

There's so much to tell. Through therapy, Rachel decided she was gay, that she could never trust men, that from the beginning penises were what screwed her up. She's taken up with Myra, who had a similar conversion.

They're happy, and together are raising their Baby Ed. Rachel's agent also represents Myra. I really get a kick when I see my old sponsor on TV and she holds up these Serenity pads for adult bladder problems. It's a good reminder of what Farmer Rob said about resentment.

Here, behind the walls, I've finally found serenity. Incarceration agrees with me. I accept things. Every day I work the Eleventh Step of HDA — prayer and meditation — and I love that Twelfth Step, carrying the message of recovery to other sick and suffering addicts. There's a huge drug problem here, and our meetings are packed.

When the lights go out and I lie in bed praying, I hear the poor suffering crackless crackerjacks crying out, "Beam me up, Scotty!" "Beam me up, Scotty!" "Beam me up, Scotty!" Again and again. "Beam me up, Scotty!" "Beam me up, Scotty!" Echoing madly along the endless rows of steel-and-cement cages like drums in the jungle. They miss Scotty's loving touch, getting out of themselves, transcending the physical, forgetting the daily grind of ego. And yeah, I'll admit it, I miss it too. What I'd give to boldly journey into space for a moment, to really let go and let God, to stop running the show, to latch onto a piece of the Rock of Ages — to have an instant spiritual awakening.

No one fucks with me here. I'm no man's punk. For that I'm grateful. My life is full. I go to meetings, work the Steps, talk to my sponsor, Father Bryan — he's getting out next month — work out, correspond with my family, friends, and fans, do my writing, and read, mostly the writings of Farmer Rob and Big Jim Williams. Step Ten tells us to continue to take a personal inventory, and to admit when we're wrong. Well, I admit it. I was wrong. I was a sick, crazy fuck, and there are moments when I have an overwhelming amount of remorse for what I've done, for taking life and hurting the families of those I killed, and that's why I stay straight and work the Steps, why I'm writing this memoir. I hope it sells, because under New York State law, the survivors of my victims receive all my earnings. I wouldn't have it any other way. I'm working that Ninth Step.

About the Ninth Step. Hunter Lodge, Jr.'s cousins and psychiatrist are contesting his will, but they don't stand a chance. It looks good for the children. Picassos and Van Goghs are fetching well over eighty million these days, so the art collection and the quarter billion in cash and holdings will go a long way toward research.

Trust Washington did not die, and he's here too, doing time for possession with intent to distribute. His physical peculiarity makes him a star in his own right. He's very popular, and he earns a lot of money in the world's oldest profession. I've tried to bring him to meetings, but he won't talk to me. Can hardly blame him. I took his Rolex. Ha ha, just a little joke. It's one of the character defects I choose to hold on to.

I'm content. Sure, there are times when I'm sad, so fucking sad I feel like shit. When the ache for Michelle and the boys is so bad I cry. Nothing worse than the ache for lost love. And when that fades, even the memory of the ache aches. I know I'm powerless over that feeling. It never really goes away. I just have to let go and let God.

What else? Oh yeah. BKA. Brutal Killers Anonymous. I founded a Twelve Step group for cold-blooded bodysnatchers. It helps. The urge for destruction and the urge to self-destruct are not so different. Father Bryan says that if we hate someone, we have to look in the mirror of our soul to see what it is about that person that reminds us of ourself.

The BKA meetings are coordinated with a victims-awareness group. The first half of the meeting, a civilian from the outside — a rape victim or someone whose significant other got killed or brutalized — talks about the feelings. Then we rap. After that the visitor leaves, and one of us tells our story; and then, like HDA, we do anniversaries and day counts and throw the meeting open. If you have a slip — kill somebody in the joint — then you're not allowed to share for ninety days after you get out of solitary. It works, it truly works. Some very notorious criminals are getting better, one day at a time.

Even me. These days I leave cookie crumbs for the cockroaches. I didn't kill anybody or anything today, and that's what The Program is all about. But you never know about tomorrow. In this place you don't know from minute to minute. I'm always ready to throw down. As the Indians say, "Hoka hey, it's a good day to die!" I still have bad moments. The other night I had a dream about putting all the world's yuppies on Nantucket Island and nuking it. Poor Nantucket. I shared that in a meeting; but we don't get many yuppies here, and if we do, well, word has it they make very good wives.

This month I've been nominated for the St. Francis of Assisi Award. (Every four weeks we give awards — sort of like Employee of the Month at McDonald's: there's the Jesus Christ Forgiveness Cup, the St. Francis Blue Ribbon for sponsoring newcomers, the Buddha Basket

of Fruit for Serenity, and the Mahatma Gandhi Passive
Resistance Dinner for Two at an Indian restaurant of
your choice in New York City, which goes to a deserving
member who gets paroled or completes his sentence —
an incentive for nonviolence.) BKA does help; but I'm a
realist. The killer inside me never really died, he's just
buried beneath layers of good works and friendliness. I'm
one retrial away from a gun and a knife and a helluva lot
of insanity. It's just like drugs and alcohol: You have to
take it one day at a time, go to meetings and drop a dime
on your disease. But don't worry, you can rest easy.
There will always be another Ed. For better or worse,
it's the Eds of the world who strike a balance.

What else? Not much. I exercise, read and write, work
in the laundry, watch TV, use the phone, go to meetings,
and talk to my sponsor and sponsees. I need the Fellowship, on a daily basis. I need to remind myself why I'm
here, what drugs and alcohol led me to. How I got here.
After all, this is my home. This is where I belong, and
more than anything else I need to belong, to be a part of
something. One day at a time, I need to reach out and
share. I need to combat the loneliness, to comfort the
fatherless child within. I need to hear myself say, "My
name is Ed, God's beloved child, and I'm feeling guilty
today."

To Weyenshet, from my heart. And thanks to Barney, Tim, Dick, Doc, Bruno, John, Derek, Max, Antonio, Joe, Helen, Bubba, Sandy, Arcade, and my family.